WHITE WRAITH

This is a work of fiction. All of the characters, organizations, and events portrayed in this novel are either products of the author's imagination or are used fictitiously.

WHITE WRAITH

A New Babel Book release
1108 S. Prairie Ave.
Sioux Falls, SD 57105

www.ShaneMoorePresents.com

ISBN 978-1-63196-035-2 (trade paperback)
Second printing.

Printed in the United States of America.

PRAISE FOR SHANE MOORE

"Shane Moore's remarkable 'Abyss Walker' novels have developed a devoted following, and for good reason. His immersive storytelling and unbridled creativity make for a winning series of page-turners."
–James Kerwin, writer/director

"Moore uses his police background to paint the thoughts of villains so accurately you begin to relate with them! I found myself pitying the monster that was directly responsible for the murder of thousands!"
–Police Writers.com

"Being an illustrator I get the opportunity to read a lot of stories so I speak from experience when I say Shane Moore's Abyss Walker series is the best! Shane's writing style is easy to read, devoid of the froo-froo found in a lot of fantasy. The insight he gives to his characters' personalities makes these books more of a study in human (and inhuman) nature than your run-of-the-mill sword and sorcery tale."
–Billy Tackett, award-winning horror artist

"From dark prophecy, to legions of undead, Shane Moore's "Abyss Walker" series is taking the fantasy world by storm!

With the detail talents of Goodkind and the story telling arc of Robert E Howard, Shane Moore has created a dark fantasy universe that will rival Tolkien. Grab some popcorn folks! The "Abyss Walker" universe is coming to a city near you!"
–Michelle Weston, Author of "A Prophecy Forgotten"

"One of the most thought out and in-depth series I have read."
–Terry Naughton, Disney

"With his Abyss Walker series Shane Moore takes his place squarely in the tradition of fantasy writers the likes of J.R.R. Tolkien and Stephen R. Donaldson. With worlds as much as part of the story as the people who inhabit them, the series seems somehow real in spite of the fantastic happenings that fill the pages. Thick, full prose with characters who come alive on the page make the series a must read."
–Sean Taylor, Gene Simmons Dominatrix

"This is definitely going to be the hottest fantasy series to date."
–Peter Mayhew, Chewbacca from Star Wars

I would like to dedicate this work to a few people; Becky, the owner of the coffee shop were I wrote this. The indomitable actor, Matt Hill, who offered his personality for Blarik. The "Biz Markie" contracted musician, Steven Tibbs, who offered his personality for the character Mr. Tibbs. And lastly, the great Sean Taylor who replied when asked if there could be a market for minotaur lead he stated; "Why not?"

...oh, and thanks to some guy named Frank Fradella.
I'm not even sure if he is a real person.

ORIGINS

TABLE OF CONTENTS

FOR MOMMA

Cries of anguish echoed in Blarik's daydream as his enemies died and fled before him. He flexed his white furcovered arms and growled menacingly: a villainous champion had emerged. Blarik circled a tall hapless mammo weed with his stick over his toddler-sized head.

"Your tyranny ends here!" Blarik rushed in, ducking under a wicked imaginary strike. With a swift motion, he brought his stick around and smacked his mighty foe. The green leafy plant broke in half and leaked white milky juice.

With his foes defeated, Blarik lifted his chin and snorted in sweet victory in the pleasant spring air. His enemy lay bleeding and his tribe was safe.

"Blarik!"

The young minotaur turned his head back across the tall kupona grass to his hut. His mother was standing out front with her hands on her hips. Kridja's harlequin fur seemed red with fury and her tail twitched angrily.

"Get your ass in here. I told you to dump that wash, not goof off!"

Blarik held his stick sword behind his back. "Yes, momma."

"The gods curse me with a stupid son like you."

Blarik dropped his stick sword and picked up the steel cooking pot. His ears drooped low and his lips quivered. He really was stupid; no wonder momma didn't love him as much as his brother, Oxtumeto. The young minotaur hoisted the pot over his shoulder and walked back to his hut. It banged and clanked off of his back with each awkward step. Maybe one day he would be as good of a son as his brother.

Blarik walked through the front door of their home. The delicious smell of cooking venison filled the air. His mother stood over a small fire and slowly turned the meat roasting on the spit.

"Put the pan over there."

Blarik nodded and set the heavy cooking pot on the flat slate rocks that surrounded a small fire pit. Kridja used a piece of black flint chip to cut carrots into small slices. The sharp rock seemed tiny in her furred meaty hands. She scooped up the carrot slices and set them on a skin. Blarik placed some kindling between the slag cooking rocks; he knew she would want to heat the stew next.

Kridja growled and slammed her fist down on top of Blarik's head. "You stupid little bug! I told you to fill the pot with water!"

Blarik's eyes teared up as he rubbed his head. "But, momma. You only told me to dump it."

Kridja snarled and hit him with the cutting rock. Blarik fell back against the hut floor. Tears welled up in his eyes and red blood dripped down his furry cheek. "But, momma.

I swear."

Kridja kicked him. "Get your ass up, you little fucker. Maybe I didn't say it, but you know we would've needed it. The gods curse me you're so stupid."

Blarik held his leg and cried. He wiped blood from his cheek and limped to his feet.

"Get!" Kridja yelled. She hurled the stew pot at him.

Blarik ducked low as the heavy metal tub whizzed overhead.

"What on earth is going on?"

Blarik looked up from his teary eyes to see his father and brother come in. They smelled of sweat and blood from, no doubt, a successful hunt. He admired his father. He was one of the best hunters in the village.

"Oh, our stupid little cow can barely follow simple tasks."

Glouwo snarled. He reached down and picked up Blarik by his horn. "Why are you such a lazy disgrace? Why can't you be more like your younger brother?"

Blarik winced. His white black horns were just beginning to form and they hurt at the stock. "I'm sorry father. I-I'll try to be better."

Glouwo tossed Blarik to the floor. "Get the pot filled or no scraps for you."

Blarik snatched up the pot and rushed out the door.

"So how was the hunt?" Kridja kissed Glouwo on the cheek.

The warrior puffed out his chest. "We did well. You should have seen Oxtumeto! His spear was fast and his aim was strong."

Kridja patted her youngest son on the head. "You're my favorite son."

Glouwo nodded. "Indeed. Tonight, you will tell the fire side story in my place."

Blarik wiped another tear from his eye as he listened from outside the hut. He liked Oxtumeto's stories. His brother was a great story teller. Why couldn't he be more like him? If he was a better hunter, maybe his father would let him go on hunts. Maybe then his father would love him. Or, even though he was embarrassed to have to stay home and do a cow's work, maybe if he was smarter, he would have remembered the water and his mother would love him more.

He looked at the seed topped lawo grass. He liked to run his furred hand over the very tops. It tickled his palms, but he didn't feel like doing it this time. Blarik kneeled down and dipped the pot in the water, careful not to stir up the dirt from the creek bed, as the fast moving stream swirled and eddied into the cooking pot.

"Whatcha doin'?"

Blarik turned to see his small pink-skinned friend. Her name was Kim, but he called her Swila. This was the first time he had seen her since last winter. "Fetching some cooking water."

"How did yak hurt your head?"

Blarik's blue eyes peered up and he wrinkled his nose. "Momma got me with the scraper. What's wrong with your chest?"

Swila squiggled her lips into the corner of her mouth. She was so ugly. No fur, no horns, and she had these gross-looking masses of inflexible flesh for ears.

"Gross. I told you not to do that around me," he groaned.

Swila giggled and did it again, but this time she crossed her eyes and stuck out her tongue. "My boobs?"

"Boobs?"

"Yea, I'm practically a woman now." She playfully poked Blarik in the ribs.

"I'm serious, Swila. I can't play. I have to get this back to momma and poppa or I'll get punished."

Swila ignored his complaints and yanked on his horn, pulling his head down. He started to protest, but her touch always made him feel at ease. "Ouch, that's one wicked gash. I think I can see your skull."

"Can you put your paste on it like last time? If I get sick from infection again and can't work, momma will be really mad."

Swila sighed and ran her hands through the tuff of white hair on Blarik's head. Blarik liked it when she did that. It made him want to sleep. She spread his fur apart and reached into her pack. She pulled out a small clay jar and stuck her fingers in it. She took the paste and spread it on Blarik's head and rubbed it in.

Blarik found it odd that she had four fingers and a thumb.

How gross it must be to have two extra fingers on each hand.

"There yak go, Blaro."

"My name is Blarik."

"Yea, but as I learn your tongue, your name sounds like white. And your fur is white."

"Don't remind me."

Swila rubbed the salve into Blarik's head. He told her about the beating he took the last time she put salve on his wounds. His mother thought he had went to the village shaman. "Why not remind you? I think your fur is handsome."

"Because, I'm the only one in the village with white fur.

It makes me different and that's bad."

"In my village, everyone tries to be different." Swila chuckled.

Blarik tried to imagine that. "I'd like to go to your village someday. I wish it wasn't so far away. I'd never make it there in time to get back for my chores."

14

A pained expression crossed her face. "Blarik, my people fear your kind. You wouldn't be welcome."

"I wish there was someone place I might go." A sadness crept over Blarik.

Swila felt her nose sting and her eyes well up with tears. "Our people fight a lot, Blarik. Your village often makes war with us."

Blarik scooped the heavy water filled tub and set it on the bank. He wrapped his arms around Swila and squeezed. He remembered how odd the embrace was when she first had given it to him, but after that it always felt good.

Swila laughed and pushed away.

"What?"

She pointed between his legs. "Your people need to invent clothes. Hugging you is awkward! Especially now that you have started getting taller."

Most of her words never made much sense to him. "You look silly in clothes. What purpose do they serve?"

"Well for starters, they cover up our naughty bits."

Blarik shook his head and rolled his eyes. He had learned it from her when she was being obstinate. It was fun.

"Don't you roll your eyes at me, Blarik Aments."

Blarik picked up the pot. "Why do you always give me two names? Only a chief would be so great as to have two names. And why do you call me wrath? I'm not mad."

"I just like to tease you."

"I have to go, Momma's gonna beat me good if I don't get back soon."

Swila's face softened. "Be careful, Blarik. Remember, I'm your friend, even when no one else is."

Blarik nodded and started back to his hut. "Meet you tomorrow?"

"I'll be here." Swila waved as she darted into the tall mammo weeds.

Blarik struggled walking home with the heavy pot of sloshing water. Sweat beaded on his nose and around his ears by the time he returned home. He entered the hut and was greeted by the smell of cooked venison. He had not eaten all day and his belly grumbled. His family sat with their legs crossed in the living area of their tent.

Oxtumeto pulled a large mouthful of cooked meat and chewed the over-sized bite. "Put that pot on the slags and don't spill any of it, you moron."

Blarik placed the heavy pot on the slags. It wasn't as hard to do as it had been in the past. Blarik smiled as he was finally getting strong like his father.

His family finished eating as Blarik sat outside the tent and watched the setting sun. His belly grumbled, but he didn't mind. When they ate it gave him a chance to enjoy some quiet time. He loved his family, but sometimes he liked sitting alone.

"Hello, Blarik."

Blarik turned to see his grandfather. The young bull leapt up and rushed over to meet him. "Grandfather!" Without thinking, Blarik wrapped his arms around the graying old bull and squeezed.

"Blarik!?"

Blarik froze. He had just done what Swila taught him.

Would his grandfather know?

"Blarik what was that?"

"I learned it from…" Blarik remembered Swila'd said his people make war with hers. He didn't want anything to happen to her. "…watching the young bulls wrestle. See how strong I'm getting?"

Werito arched an eyebrow of skepticism. He reached into his pack and handed Blarik some dried meat. "Eat boy. I know how your parent's treat you."

Blarik munched on the meat. It was dry and salty, but good.

"Blarik, I want you to stop seeing the human girl."

"I…"

"She has nothing to fear from me. Let's take a walk."

Blarik nodded and resumed eating, though the worried sensation in his belly made him feel sick. "How did you know, Grandpa?"

"Blarik, I have been watching you closely since you were born. You're something special."

16

Blarik felt that pit in his stomach get worse. "Grandpa, you won't hurt her will you?"

Werito shook his head. "No, child. But, our people would. She makes a great risk coming here day after day in the summer. I see how you have become friends with her."

"Why would we hurt her? Or make war with her. She is nice. And smart!"

Werito rubbed Blarik's tuff of fur. "Her people are fearful of us. We are bigger, stronger, and we have feuded with them since my grandfather was a calf. Because they attack us, we make sure and attack them. Keep them afraid, and keep them in their walled villages."

"They have walled villages?"

His grandfather nodded. "Blarik, I want you to listen carefully. There is an important meeting coming up about you."

"With my da?"

"Yes, and with the village council."

"About what?"

"It doesn't matter right now. Can you keep a secret, Blarik?"

"Sure, why?"

"Just promise me that if I tell you to leave the village, you will be ready with no questions asked."

Blarik nodded. He felt tears beginning to well up in his eyes, but he didn't want to be weak in front of his grandpa so he fought them back.

Werito patted his head. "Good, boy. Be ready, Blarik. The time may be at hand tomorrow night."

Blarik watched his grandfather turn and walk back toward his hut. What did that mean? Was he about to be banished? He had finally done it. His family had enough of him. Why did he have to be so worthless? Blarik growled and stomped the ground. Why did he have to be such a failure?

***

"What do you want, Greybull?" Glouwo snarled to his father. "Come to talk more of your stupid old words?"

"I've come to plead with you one last time. Reconsider. Blarik is a fine boy. Prophecy be damned, he just wants you to love him."

"Piss on that disgrace." Glouwo spit on the ground. "He has brought our family much shame!"

"How? Because he has white fur? Don't be stupid, son. He is twice the size of the other young bulls. The old words ring true."

Kridja spit at Werito's feet. "Piss on you, old bull. Sacrificing him to Kaph is the only thing that can give this family some respect. Imagine how you would have felt had Glouwo been born with white fur? You would have bled him dry with your own knife!"

Werito nodded. "I was young and foolish then. I didn't know about the old words like I do now. Blarik is special. Go to the elders tomorrow and stand with me to spare him. If we stood together, we could sway them."

Kridja snarled. "Don't you dare, old bull. You're meddling has done enough already."

"Shut your mouth, Jegino, the cow." Werito backhanded Kridja, and she fell to her backside.

Glouwo sprung in fury. His fist struck Werito in the snout, knocking him back into the tent wall, tearing a portion of it down with him.

Blarik turned to see the commotion. His father was kicking and stomping his grandfather.

"No!" Blarik ran toward them. "Stop! Please!"

Glouwo stomped furiously. "How dare you strike my woman, old bull! I'll stomp you into butter paste!"

Blarik felt something new in his heart: something powerful, something dangerous. He loved his father, but he loved his grandfather too. With a full charge, Blarik lowered his head and collided with Glouwo. His thick skull and tiny horn buds struck home.

The blow knocked Glouwo prone. "I'll bleed you for that!" Werito kicked the tent flap off of himself. Blood dripped from his nose and eye as he placed his fingers together. The old bull said a strange word that

Blarik had never heard. Great fingers of earth ripped up and wrapped themselves around his father's waist and legs. Glouwo struggled against the magically animated rock and dirt, but could not move.

"This is not over, old bull!" Glouwo said and then pointed to Blarik. "I will go to the elders and this disgrace will be gone by the morrow's eve!"

Blarik felt his heart sink. They did plan to kick him out of the family. Shame overwhelmed him. He ran into the night. He ran as fast as his legs would carry him. Tears streamed down his white cheeks and the cool night air rushed by his ears. He ran for miles, past the creek and toward Swila's home. After several hours, he stopped to rest under a thick oak tree. His barrel chest heaved as he sucked in great gasps of air. He was going to be banished from his family. Soon, he would have no one. Is that what his grandfather meant?

Why didn't they love him? Why couldn't he be as good at hunting as his brother? Why couldn't he do better when cooking with his mother? His father was right; he was nothing but a disgrace.

The cold spring night brought chills, but the sound of crickets and frogs soothed the young Minotaur's mind. Just before he was about to fall asleep—it hit him. His blue eyes shot wide open as he sat up. Why didn't he think of this before!?

His father didn't love him because he was a bad hunter, and his mother didn't love him because he was terrible in the kitchen. But, if he could make a hunter's spear, travel to the Steam Flats, he could kill a mighty salt crab. His mother loved salt crabs and such a difficult kill would not only earn his family much honor with the villages, it would make both of his parents love him!

Blarik smiled and drifted off to sleep. Tomorrow, he would redeem himself and finally be loved!

THE TIP OF THE SPEAR

Blarik opened his eyes. His head was being cradled by Swila as she rubbed his head and hummed a tune.

"Good morning, sleeping bull."

Blarik looked up at her, and smiled. "I dreamt of you."

"Why are you so far away from your home?"

Blarik sat up and yawned. "It was terrible. My grandfather got into a fight with my da. My family is going to banish me."

Swila placed her hand on his arm. "I'm so sorry, Blaro."

"Last night I figured out what I need to do."

Swila laid her head on Blarik's shoulder. His fur was soft. "I'll help you, whatever it is."

Blarik patted her head. "It's nothing you can help me with. It's a bull's work."

"Oh. What is this bull's work?"

Blarik got to his feet. "First, I will craft a mighty spear. Then I will go to the Steam Flats and kill a salt crab. That will make my family love me. Only the greatest warriors can kill a salt crab, so it will bring my family much honor and they won't banish me."

"First things first. Put this on." Swila reached into her pack.

Blarik looked down. "What is that?"

She held up a flap of leather with a belt and another flap on the other side. "It's a loin cloth."

Blarik sniffed at it. "Smells like hide to me."

"No silly, it's just called that."

"What's it for?"

Swila laughed and pointed between Blarik's legs. "It's for covering up that."

Blarik frowned and looked down. "Why?"

"Blarik, my people hide our bodies. We don't like to be naked."

"But you're not. You wear clothes."

Swila chuckled. "But you are not." "But I'm not one of your people!"

"Yea, but. …it's just intimidating."

"Okay, Swila. I'll wear it for you."

Swila smiled and helped fasten it around his waist. "Thank you. So, when do we leave for this hunt?"

Blarik shook his head. "No, this hunt is for bulls. Not cows."

"Blarik, with my people, many warriors are women."

"Are you trying to be a warrior too?"

Swila shyly slid a lock of her long brown hair behind her ear. "Something like that."

"I would be happy to help you earn the respect of your family, Swila. Then we both will be loved."

"So, what now?"

"First I need to make a spear."

Blarik sniffed at a few small saplings. He pulled on them gently and bent their trunks. "I've seen my father do this once."

Swila chuckled. "Of course, you want one that is thick enough to offer flexibility, but not thick enough to be so rigid it will break."

Blarik narrowed his blue eyes. "Your people make spears?"

"Blarik, weapons of war are not just known to your tribe." The cool spring breeze blew Swila's brown hair about her face. "My people wear armor too."

"Armor?"

"It's like a hide, but made of steel."

"Steel?"

Swila chuckled. "Do you know anything of war? I figured your village would have been teaching you about such things by now."

Blarik hung his head. "No, I am a disgrace to my family. I'm not allowed to hunt, or make spears, or even cook with momma."

Swila placed a comforting arm on his warm, furry shoulder. "I'm pretty good at scurrying up a rabbit and hitting it with a short spear."

Blarik nodded. "So do you know how to make one?"

"Well, I've never really made one. But, I have seen it done."

Blarik arched an eyebrow and smiled. The afternoon breeze came in waves across the tall Lawo grass as he and Swila walked toward the creek. Blarik enjoyed his time with Swila. He liked not being yelled at. She made him feel like he was good. Not a disgrace.

"We should be coming up on some saplings as the creek widens." Swila said.

"What's wrong with the other saplings?"

"They were too thick. The spear penetrates by its slenderness and its point. Not by its weight."

Blarik stepped over an old log washed up from a past flood. "My father made thick spears. Much thicker than the ones we looked at."

Swila roughly rubbed the top of Blarik's head. "Your people make spears to crack through the metal armor of their enemies."

"But the crabs have armor. It's their shell."

Swila smiled. "But, we want to hit them in the vital areas between their shells."

Blarik pondered the thought for a moment. He had never actually seen a salt crab. But, he wasn't going to admit that to Swila. "Right, but I was thinking just in case."

"Well, I tell you what. Your spear will be bigger than mine. Even though we are the same height, your hands are thicker, so your spear will be too."

Blarik ran his hands across the top of the Lawo grass. Its tassels tickled his palm. He inhaled the wet creek bed breeze and listen to Swila talk. "I don't want to go back."

"Huh?"

Blarik growled and ran toward the creek. His heavy white hooves thundered into the ground. Just as he reached the edge of the creek bed, he leapt high into the air and let out a tremendous yell. "HOOOWHAAYA!"

Swila watched in astonishment as her normally demure friend ran and jumped from the edge of the creek. He outstretched his furry arms and tossed his head back. His thick white body disappeared from under the depths of the creek in a tremendous splash. She ran to the edge of the creek. Laughter overcame her. "Blaro!"

Blarik erupted from the surface. His wet white hair was smashed to his head and his blue eyes beamed. Water dripped from his horn sprouts. "I'm never going back!"

"Blarik, where will you go?"

The young bull took in a mouthful of water and spit it at Swila. "Anywhere. I feel alive!"

Swila glanced around nervously. Her new friend's revelations were dangerous. She knew he wasn't treated well at home, but he would not be safe outside his village. "Blarik, aren't you going to impress your dad and your mom?"

Blarik swam to the shore. He laid on his belly in the muddy beach and kicked his legs in the water. "I want to. But, I already missed chores today. Besides, they hate me, anyway."

Swila leaned down at the edge of the creek. She sat down on the grassy shore. "Blaro, it wouldn't be safe. Your people would target you. Mine would too."

Blarik lowered his furry chin into the mud. The weight of his heavy head pushed down creating a tiny mud dike. "I guess they would. But, I don't care. I'm going to hunt this crab. I'm going to kill it for my mother and to show my hunting prowess for to my father. But, one way or another, I'm not going back to stay."

She climbed down in the muddy beach and set next to Blarik. She ran her hands through the tuff of fur on top of his head. "I'll help you how I can."

Blarik jumped up and grabbed Swila by the arms, startling her. Blarik hoisted her over his shoulder and with a grin tossed her into the air. She kicked and giggled as she was hurled through the air before splashing into the cool creek water.

Swila surfaced, "Blaro! You freaked me out."

Blarik chuckled. "Today is not a day for being sad. I won't have it."

Swila giggled and splashed playfully at Blarik. The growing minotaur covered his face and sneezed. He hated getting water up his nose. Each time he sneezed, Swila laughed louder and splashed harder. Blarik ran from the creek and onto the grassy shore. "No splashing. It gets in my nose."

Swila swam closer to the shore. "Ah, whets matter? Big tough bull afraid of a little water?"

Blarik laughed and sprinted toward Swila. She tried to turn and swim back out, but it was too late. Blarik leaped and tucked his knees to his chest. "Boulder ball!"

***

"Where is the little bastard?" Kridja screamed. "He will ruin everything!"

Glouwo kicked a clay pot. His heavy hoof shattered it, "This is your fault. You should have been watching him."

"My fault?" Kridja doubled up her fist. "If you had not been digging dirt with your father, maybe you would have seen him run off!"

Glouwo snorted. "That old shaman is weak. There was no dirt digging, only him feeling the power of my fist!"

Kridja waved her hand in dismissal. "Even now, on the verge of our ultimate shame, you want to argue a bull's fool."

"I can track him. If I get him back by the ceremony, our family won't be shamed."

Kridja pondered the idea. The tribe had agreed to sacrifice Blarik to their god, Kaph. It was to be at sunset. This would bring their tribal standing up high. Maybe even earn Glouwo a seat at the elder table. "So what, we tell the elders nothing?"

Glouwo nodded. He grabbed Kridja by her arms. "It's risky, but if we go to them now, they will learn of Blarik's disobedience. That will most likely be a bad omen to the elders."

Kridja nodded her head in agreement. "How will you track him?"

"I am friends with Old Anku. Maybe he will let me use one of his Morwen."

Kridja shuddered. "Those horrid monsters should be put down."

"I don't care for them, or Anku's dark magic, but if that's what it takes to get Blarik's no good filthy carcass to bleed before the council, then it has to be done."

Kridja nodded distantly. "Just make sure he comes back alive. I'll not be shamed by your failure."

Glouwo rubbed his meaty hands on Kridja's arms. Her soft Harlequin fur roused him. He snorted and wrapped his powerful arms forcefully around her. He felt her pulse quicken. She pressed her body against his and bit his neck. "Tell me how the boy will bleed while you have your way with me."

Glouwo grabbed her by her hair and pulled her head. He forced her to her back and bit at her ear. "First thing I will do to the little fuck is…"

***

Blarik and Swila laid on their backs in the warm afternoon sun. She pressed her body alongside his. "You know, Blaro. I really enjoy being here with you…"

"Look, that one looks like a Morwen." Blarik pointed to an odd shaped cloud.

"What's that?"

Blarik shuddered. "It's this awful crab monster that Anku keeps."

"What does he do with them?"

"The elders use them to hunt down our enemies or those that break tribal law."

Swila felt a gnawing fear growing in her belly. "Would running away be breaking one of those laws?" "Nah, that's a family issue." Swila sighed in relief.

"No, you would have to be a killer or something for them to come after you with a Morwen."

26

Swila squeezed Blarik's hand. "We need to get moving. The salt flats are several hours away and we have not even made spears yet."

Blarik stood and brushed the dry grass from his legs. He readjusted his loincloth and double-checked it. He kind of liked the absurd clothing. It made him feel like he was in a battle costume or some ceremonial outfit like the elders wore.

Swila gathered up her things and tied them tight to the back of her belt. "Let's head to that thicket over there. I bet those saplings will work nice."

Blarik swished his tail and entered the small thicket. The numerous saplings were clumped close together and he imagined this must be what it was like to be a rabbit moving through the lawo grass. Sunlight poked through the leafy thicket canopy in small numerous beams.

"I like it here, Swila. Maybe this is why rabbits like to hid in the lawo grass."

She tugged on a sapling and bent it slightly. She placed her thumb along the width. "That's a good match for me. I didn't think there would be any here that are my size."

Blarik peered up at the sun as he moved between the saplings and wondered if the low snakes ever peered up at the sun like this.

Swila pulled her knife from her boot and chopped at the base of the sapling. In a few whacks, she cut through.

"What's that?"

"My knife?" Swila held it forward.

"No, the stone. It's really smooth."

"This is steel, Blaro. This is what I mean when I describe it."

Blarik awkwardly took the knife in his hands and tried to bend it. The blade did not flex. The boyish minotaur ran his thumb along the side. "It's so smooth and hard. What did you use to shape it?"

Swila frowned. "What do you mean? Like what forge did we use?"

"Forge? Is that the base rock?"

"No, a forge is a super-hot fire pit where our blacksmith's melt the steel. Then when it's molten, they hammer and shape it while it cools.

I've seen my father do it a few times. It's pretty neat. The sparks fly up like moon bugs."

Blarik sniffed the steel. It was like nothing he had ever smelled. "It kinda smells funny."

"That's the oil."

"Oil?"

"Yea, oil. It keeps the blade from rusting."

"Rusting?"

Swila sighed. "We don't have all day. I'll tell you about it as we go." Blarik reluctantly gave the knife back to Swila.

"Okay, Blaro. I think this sapling will be suited for you." She pulled on it until it was leaning over. Blarik stuck his thumb next to it. "Yep, perfect. Now, bend it over so I chop it easier."

Blarik bent the sapling over and Swila chopped at it. It took more whacks, but she eventually made it through the sapling's trunk.

"Now, peel the branches and leaves away while I go gather some grass to start our fire."

Blarik nodded. Swila knew so many things. She was so smart. His father never taught him how to make a spear, but she knew. And she was a girl. He was just now realizing how much of a disgrace he was to his family.

The smell of fresh smoke filled the thicket. Blarik liked the smell. It reminded him of cooking fires and his belly grumbled. "I'm hungry. I hope we can hurry."

Swila opened her small leather pack and handed Blarik a biscuit. "Here. Eat a few of these. My mother made them for me."

Blarik sniffed the odd shaped roll. It looked like a soft brown rock.

"Just eat it, Blaro." Swila broke sticks and placed them in the growing fire.

Blarik placed one in his mouth. He chewed slowly at first, then he chewed more piously. "Viss ith goooood!"

Swila giggled. "Momma makes the best around!"

Blarik nodded in agreement. "It tastes like honey."

"Yep, momma makes a honey icing that she spreads on them right when they're done."

Blarik took small bites from the other one and tried to make it last. When he finished, he licked his fingers and wondered Why would Swila come with him? She had a great mother, and father.

"Okay, while I grab some more wood to get the fire going, you need to take my knife and sharpen the tips. Make them into a point." Swila pulled her knife and forcefully threw it down, sticking it in the soft earth, blade first.

Blarik's eyes widened. He picked up the knife and mimicked her. It took him a couple of times, but he was able to master the simple throw in no time. Swila was surely a mighty hunter. Blarik sat down and went to task. He had seen his father do this before. He set the spear at an angle and brought the knife down. It was much sharper than any stone weapon his village had. When Blarik had finished forming the tips, he went back to throwing the knife into the dirt.

Swila returned and added more logs to the fire.

"Watch this." Blarik said with pride. He tossed the knife end over end and stuck it in the dirt. "I added a twirl to it."

Swila smiled. "Some of our warriors can throw these through the air from a distance to stick in our enemies."

What a sight that would be to behold! It didn't take him long to remember that his people often warred with hers. He thought of one of the warriors throwing that knife at him. He rubbed his chest and made a pained look while he imagined what it would be like to have the knife plunge into him. Blarik shook his head.

"I think the fire is hot enough. Now, we need to harden the tips. But, if we were hunting fish, we would cut barbs first." Blarik nodded; he had seen his brother's barbed spear.

Swila slowly turned the spear tips in the fire, slowly blackening them. "We do this to make the fire get the water out, Blaro. It makes the wood harder. But, we can't do it too long, or it will be brittle."

"How do you know when it has been in the fire long enough?"

"I figure as long as the outside is blackened a little that ought to be good enough."

Blarik burned the tip of his spear with Swila's help. When they were finished, he smiled. He had made his first ever spear.

He wondered if his father would have been proud.

HUNTERS AND THEIR PREY

"Come in." Anku's raspy voice clamored from inside the dark hut.

Glouwo lifted the flap and walked inside, his movements uneasy and fearful.

"Why do you seek out, Anku?" The thin frail minotaur shifted in the shadows. His gray hair had yellowed with age.

"I have a brigand that has run off with one of my family's possessions. If he isn't returned, it will bring my family much shame."

The old bull puffed on a long thin pipe that sent snake like smoke tendrils into the air. "A real tragedy to lose something so valuable."

"Yes. Yes it is. This is why I seek your help."

"Do you know how to control a Morwen?" "I do not." Glouwo coughed.

Anku chuckled and then burst into a coughing fit of his own. His frail body heaved violently. His yellowed hand pulled a cork on a waterskin. The old bull sipped to calm his cough. "I need a possession of the thief. Did he leave anything behind?"

Glouwo nodded. He had heard the Morwen tracked by scent. "I have this bit of cloth."

The old bull reached out as his milky eyes examined the fabric. "Looks like bedding."

"Perhaps from his bedroll. Rogues no doubt live on the run." His sunken lifeless eyes made Glouwo uneasy

"Rogues also live in huts."

Glouwo felt his heart race. Did Anku know? Would he tell the Elders? "So, how much?"

Anku's withered lips crept into a smile. "Forty crwo."

"That's half a season's worth!"

"If you want Morwen, you will pay." Anku slinked back into his comfy chair.

Glouwo snorted and ran his hands through his hair and stared at the ground. Forty daily rations of grain would mean he would have to work harder in their garden to make sure his family could get through the colder months. "Fine."

"This way to the Morwen pits." Anku groaned as he stood up.

The old minotaur lifted a rear tent flap revealing a long dark cave. He snatched up a withered old cane and limped his way down the passage, Glouwo wrinkled his nose at the smell. The odor of decaying flesh hung in the air like a thick fog.

"Don't mind the smell, they like their meat ripe." Anku chuckled.

Glouwo followed for several minutes before the small passage opened into a larger room. Three bulbous forms lounged in a shallow pit. They were covered in long nasty looking spines, much like a porcupine and with ten or so insect-like legs. Their heads were small and wolf shaped with two huge mandibles protruding out like a stag beetle. Their tails were long and narrow and wrapped around their bodies in an odd position and seemed to slither like a snake when they moved.

Anku chuckled at Glouwo's expression. "Never seen a Morwen before?"

Glouwo shook his head. "No."

The old necromancer grunted as he started down the stairs into the pit. "Their collars are enchanted by the shamans to make 'em friendly. Otherwise they would rip you apart."

"Where do you get them?"

Anku turned with a sinister look in his clouded eyes. "Don't worry about where I get them. Just know I can get more anytime."

Glouwo nodded. He was beginning to think this might have been a bad idea.

Anku unhooked one of the Morwen's chains. He gently patted the beast on its armored head and stroked the tiny quills that splayed backwards. "I will accept payment now."

32

Glouwo took a deep breath and loosed his pack. He counted out forty of the forty-seven bags he'd brought. Anku eyed them hungrily before placing them in his knapsack. "You will need to keep a hold of the Morwen's leash at all times. If you sleep, you will need to tie her to a tree. If you want your prey alive, do not let your Morwen within ten yards. Even her tail can whip out and snatch up prey."

Glouwo timidly took hold of the chain leash. Anku kneeled and placed the bit of cloth down in front of the beast. He whispered something in its ear. The Morwen perked up.

Its quills splayed out and its long serpentine tail slid around its body excitedly.

Anku smiled. "She is ready. Go out the far passage to the valley and start there. She will be able to track your prey for about ten miles consistently. Up to twenty fairly well, so if your quarry is headed far, you better hurry."

Glouwo nodded nervously. This had better work; he had invested so much.

***

Blarik and Swila followed the rivulet south. Several tributaries had fed into the small creek, making it twice as wide as it was when they started. The small rocky peaks to the east and west seemed to narrow and meet about a mile or so ahead. Blarik could see large clouds of steam rising up just on the other side of the rocky ridge.

Swila moved fairly easy over the rocky shoreline, but Blarik's hard hooves made him slide. He had a hard time getting a solid footing, falling several times. "These rocks are too slippery."

Swila chuckled. "If your feet weren't like your horns, it would be easier."

Blarik rubbed his sore elbow. "I'm getting in the water."

"Okay, Blaro. I have to wear shoes and wet feet are not good to travel in. So, I'll see on the other side of the pass." Swila shrugged.

Blarik nodded and waded into the creek. The current was slow moving, but fast enough he didn't need to swim. The white bull floated on his back and marveled at the tall dark rocky cliffs. Long tendrils of brown and green moss clung to their surface and dozens of white birds dipped in and out.

The creek slowly winded for a mile or so, until it cleared the small mountain pass. The land on the other side was alien to him. The creek emptied out into several small channels that led to gray muddy flats. Steam and bubbles erupted from the pools that lay near a dead forest. The trees were all black husks with a sparse limb here and there. They were crusted with white and yellow crystals that made their way to the tops. The air stunk like rotting eggs and it burned Blarik's nose. He swam to the shore and carefully climbed out onto the banks as Swila navigated the rocks to avoid stepping in the mud.

"This is one hell of a nasty place." Swila scrunched her nose.

"No wonder salt crabs are so hard to get."

Swila placed her hand on Blarik's shoulder for balance and hopped to the rock next to him. "Look, Blaro. You can see the ocean from here."

Blarik squinted his eyes and gazed to the south. "I don't see anything other than that long blue hill on the horizon."

"That's the ocean!" Swila giggled and leapt down into the mud, ignoring the warm gooey mess. "Come on!"

She pulled Blarik by his arm. His heavy hooves sunk deep into the mud and he struggled to keep up..

Blarik grabbed Swila by the arm and forced her to stop.

His heavy nose sniffed the air.

"What is it, Blaro?"

"I smell something. Something odd."

"Like what? A salt crab?"

"Like I know what they smell like. Maybe you farted?"

Swila punched him in the arm. "We need to hurry and get your crab. I have to go soon."

Blarik thought about spending the night alone again. He would miss his friend. "I don't know where these things are. I've just seen Momma eat them."

Swila tugged on Blarik's arm again. "Well, most crabs live in the ocean. So I expect these do too."

Blarik followed Swila for many minutes. The ocean was the largest thing he had ever seen. It extended from horizon to horizon. One great expansion of water. "It's beautiful!"

"My village lives on it, to the east. A few days from here.

But, my farm is pretty close."

Blarik nodded. "I'd like to see your farm someday."

"Maybe at night when no one could see you, but the same reason you can't bring me to your village is the same reason I can't bring you to mine."

"Maybe if you told them I was nice, and how I can work hard."

"No, they still would be afraid of you. Blaro, you are small now, but you will grow big. Real big."

Blarik lowered his ears. He just didn't fit in anywhere. He glanced back to the salt flats. The bubbling swamp sat just a bit lower than the beach but he didn't see anything that would hold a large salt crab. The beach had nothing either. "I don't see anything that even resembles a crab. Thanks for your help, but I think my hunt failed."

Swila patted Blarik's shoulder. "Well, we made some fine spears, had we seen any."

Blarik smiled. "Yes we did. And you taught me how to make them."

The pair wrestled and played on the beach for several hours. They kept an eye out looking for a crab, but found little more than the diminutive sand crab. The afternoon sun began its descent toward the west.

"We need to get back, Blaro."

"Yea. I'll take you back to the other side of the rock ridge. I think I'll camp there tonight. Will you come see me tomorrow?"

"Sorry, Blaro. I have to help dad with the chickens tomorrow. But I can come the next day."

Blarik put his arm around Swila. He liked how he felt when she was next to him. They walked back into the salt flats. "Okay, Kim."

"Blarik! You never call me by my real name."

"It's okay, you prolly like that name better." Blarik bent over. "Now hop on my back. I'll carry you over the mud."

Swila hopped on. She giggled as Blarik stomped through the hot clay mud. "Nah, Blaro. I like Swila. It's my minotaur name."

Blarik carried her as swiftly as he could. She was much lighter than the stew pot of water he normally carried for his mother. He jumped to one particular smooth looking area. The mud was dry and there was a hard rock under it. Blarik paused to rest. Swila hopped from his back.

"Did you feel that?" Swila looked down.

The ground erupted from under them. The rock shifted and rose, knocking both of them prone. Blarik landed in the thick mud and Swila landed on her feet. Both watched in awe as the rock rose from the sulfurous mud on four spindly chitin legs.

Blarik struggled to catch his breath. He got to his feet in the cumbersome mud and grabbed his spear. "It's a salt crab!"

Swila stood in awe. The beast's body was the size of two full-grown Minotaur's and its spindle legs placed it as tall as one too. It had two massive pinchers, but one was twice the size of the other. It looked like it could cut a horse in half.

"Swila, your spear!"

Swila glanced down at her spear. The weapon seemed so tiny and useless against the monstrous crab.

Blarik skipped forward and let his spear fly. The heavy weapon soared through the air and bounced harmlessly off of the crab's armor.

Swila watched the beast slowly move sideways through the mud and away. Its movements were mesmerizing.

"Some help you were." Blarik passed her and picked up his spear.

"Blaro! Did you not see the size of that thing? It was annoyed at us. Had it know you were trying to kill it with your spear, it would have prolly cut us in half."

Blarik watched the crab meander several dozen yards before settling down into the mud again. "Well, I aim to kill it. I'm not going to prove my father right." He marched toward the crab. "I'm NOT a disgrace."

Swila felt a worry in her stomach. Were all boys the same? Human or Minotaur, when it came to proving something, they seemed ridiculously stubborn about the task. "Blaro, don't be bull headed."

Blarik turned. "What?"

Swila thought about what she said, "I mean, don't be stubborn. Look, being a disgrace has nothing to do with killing that dangerous crab. You were not a disgrace before you killed one, and you won't be if you don't."

Blarik shook his head. "No, I set out to do this. If I fail, that will make me a disgrace."

Swila struggled to catch up in the hot mud. Gouts of stinging steam hung in the air. "Seriously? Blarik there is no way you can kill that thing. I'm not even sure you can hurt it."

Blarik wiped the mud from his spear on a dead tree. Bits of yellow and white crystals cleaned the handle. The young bull wiped his hands on his hips and tested the grip. He seemed to be able to grip the wooden shaft nicely.

"Blarik, please. Don't do this. I don't want to watch you get killed."

Blarik stood on a small muddy ridge, just above the embedded salt crab. He took a deep breath. His grandfather had taught him about clearing his mind and concentrating when he needed to do something. So Blarik thought about the sunset. He focused on the picture of the setting sun. The bright orange ball in the western sky dipped low. Lower. Lower. The sun was now gone and the evening sky darkened quickly. Blarik watched the vision fade from his mind until there was little to be seen, then blackness. His bright blue eyes rocketed open. Blarik leapt from the small muddy ridge. The wind ripped through his white fur. He gripped his spear in the middle as his heavy hooves touched down on the back of the salt crab; he drove his spear home. The sharp wooden weapon crashed through the hard shell. The crab shot out of the mud. Dark blue ooze poured from the around the spear. Blarik struggled to keep his footing. His hooves had little grip. With a final groan, Blarik shoved the spear deeper into the crab. The great beast skittered through the mud, knocking over blackened trees sending a shower of yellow and white crystals into the air. As abruptly as the crab rocketed to life, it toppled over. Blarik tumbled headlong into a steam pool. The young bull got to his feet and stared at his handiwork. He wiped the stinging salt water from his eyes. There before him was the dead carcass of a giant salt crab, felled by his single spear. Blarik felt an overwhelming since of relief and accomplishment wash over him. "I did it!"

Swila came running and hopping. She waved her spear in the air. "Blarik, you did it! You really did it!"

Blarik pointed at the dead crab. "I told you! I told you I could!"

Swila threw down her spear and jumped into Blarik's arms. The force of her body knocked him back into the mud. "I'm so proud of you Blaro!"

Blarik stared into her eyes. So brown, so soft and caring. They were nothing like his mother's eyes. "I couldn't have done it had you not taught me how to use a spear."

Swila wiped a bit of mud from Blarik's face. She had always thought him ugly when they'd first met, but he was pretty. His eyes seemed so human to her, so blue, and peaceful.

"You can get off me now."

Swila blushed. "Sorry."

Blarik got to his feet and held his arms out in disgust.

"I'm covered in this mud and nasty water. I need to wash off."

Swila nodded. "I can stay a bit longer, but then I need to go back."

Blarik felt his joy sink. He had just killed a salt crab with the spear he made. His father would probably love him now.

But, he would trade it all for another day with his friend. "Don't worry, Blaro." Swila punched him in the arm. "I'll be back the day after tomorrow."

"Well, can you help drag this thing to the rocks? I need to cut it up and get it ready to take home."

"Okay, Blaro. Why are you going to take it home?"

38

"I need to know if da and momma really will love me or if I am just too much of a screw up to be loved."

Swila glanced over at the monstrous beast. It clearly weighed several hundred pounds. Maybe even a thousand. "Blaro, are you going to cut it all up? I don't think you will make it home tonight if you do."

Blarik took a deep breath. "No. But, I think when I do come home, my parents will be so happy that I'm safe and see what I have done, they will forgive me."

Swila bit her lip doubtfully. "Well, you better use my knife or this will take even longer."

A FAMILY MATTER

The waning sun sent waves of fury through Glouwo. If he didn't get that damned white bastard before the council tonight, he would likely lose any chance he had of reclaiming family honor.

The Morwen moved at a relentless pace. Its many legs skittered over the land while its tail wove around itself making the beast's quills perform an eerie dance. The monster led him along the riverbanks. Glouwo thought the beast inept until he came across a small camp near some saplings. He noticed some small minotaur tracks in the mud, but what confused the great bull, were the other signs. Saplings had been cleaved by something sharp. Something much like the tools of man. And then the most precarious sign, the saplings were molded into spears. The ones chosen were much too small to be for any minotaur, but why did human's need spears? Were they making traps? And why did they have Blarik? Glouwo imagined how he would kill them all if Blarik was dead. How was he to sacrifice him to Kaph if the bastard had already died?

Glouwo made his way to the edge of the river where it sliced its way through the small rocky ridge. The Morwen sniffed around the edge of the rocky shore. Its thick pincher like mandibles clicked. Glouwo couldn't tell if the beast even had a nose. It simply placed its head down and probed the ground with two small feelers with dandelion looking hairs on them.

Glouwo held on to the Morwen's chain as tight as he could as the beast led him over the rocky beach alongside the creek. The Morwen scampered over the slippery rocks with ease, but Glouwo struggled. His hard hooves did not allow him great footing. The bull was amazed at what he saw when he cleared the other side. The salt flats were more spectacular than he had imagined. Gouts of steam and gas bubbled from gray water mud pits. The trees were all dead, covered with a sulfurous and salty crystal mix. The creek was practically even with the flats, so a perpetual flow of water fed into the hot murky mess. The air stung Glouwo's nose and made his eyes water. For the first time since they left, the Morwen did not pull on the chain. It stood there motionless. Its tiny feelers bounced up and down on the mud furiously, but it did not move.

It dawned on Glouwo why the humans came here. The inner earth's bubbling would make it impossible for them to be tracked passed this point. These humans were crafty. Glouwo glanced to the setting sun. He would most likely not make it back in time. Someone was going to pay.

***

Blarik groaned and tossed the empty crab lag section into the pile next to him. The meat was not like he expected. It was runny and slimy. He wasn't sure how to dry it out, or if he even could. He didn't have any salt and using the monster's brains like his father had used before wouldn't work, since he couldn't even find the thing's brain. He had roasted the meat he collected over the fire. It cooked down to a smooth white. It smelled sweet and Blarik couldn't wait to eat some.

He had fashioned a fair sized carrying case out of the crab shell. Blarik was pretty proud of himself. As he watched the western sky, he was amazed at the yellows and oranges that could be seen from the salt flats. There were no trees or mountains to take away from the view. Aside from a few scraggly dead tree trunks, the sky was clear and free. He loved the sunset.

Blarik sighed. He missed his grandfather. The young bull sat in silence until the sun finally passed behind the veil of the world. Blarik snapped back to his task. There was a lot of crabmeat to cook.

***

"Where is your bull?"

Kridja shuffled uneasily before the council. "Uh, he is, um. He is looking for the bastard child."

Whispers and deep growls of judgment echoed in the elder hut. "You lost the anomaly?"

Kridja glanced around. She could feel the judging eyes of the tribe. They thought her a failure for birthing such a monstrosity. Some even said she lay with a demon to produce such a hideous offspring. "Glouwo is hunting him."

The elders sat back in their wooden chairs, some folded their arms, and others rolled their eyes. "We expected such a debacle from your shameful family."

"Do not tarry with your judgments, but blame lies not on the shoulder of Jegino, or her rotten womb."

The elders watched with earnest as Anku walk into the hut. The scraggly old bull's gray coat was stained yellow from his smoke habit and his horns brown. He walked slowly with a withered wooden cane. His dull sightless eyes darted about the room.

"What say you, Anku? How do you speak on the behalf of this Jegino?"

Anku took his seat as medicine man. "Glouwo came to me this afternoon."

Kridja felt her heart sink. Why had the fool consorted with the necromancer? "Elders, surely my husband would not consort with Anku over a family matter."

Anku growled. "Surely you would not call that spawn of your demonic womb that this village raised a family matter. That bastard child is a curse to us all."

The elders nodded. "Agreed. We have had dry season after dry season since his birth."

Anku frowned. "Jegino, were is your bull's father? Where is Werito?"

"Surely he is with my husband, returning the white bastard to us." Kridja shuffled nervously.

Anku harrumphed. "Clearly not. He made his opinion of the demon spawn quite clear last meeting. I would argue that he likely took the boy in some desperate attempt to keep us from spilling his blood."

Kridja glanced around. Could this be true, could she be saved from this shame by the bungling decision of Glouwo's ridiculous father?

The Elders leaned back in their wooden chairs in thought. Kridja did not miss her opportunity. "I believe the witchdoctor is right. My husband didn't share with me why he was setting out, other than Blarik was missing."

Anku chuckled. "You named the bastard? That was a foolish thing to do."

Several of the elders chuckled. "Look at the Jegino. Her heart is as cold mountain snow. What other mother could distance herself from such a disgusting offspring? I don't fault her for naming the beast. It shows us the power in her resolve." "Aye, I believe her words," another elder chimed in.

The Rigjo stood. The others quieted before the tribe chief. His massive bulk towered over the others and the gray hairs on his chin shook as he spoke. "It's settled. We shall give Glouwo time to return with the spawn. When is his tenth year, Kridja?"

Kridja lowered her head. It was difficult to look into the blue eyes of the great chief. He had been the only minotaur known to have blue eyes. "His tenth will come this week."

Rigjo nodded. "We have time. But, we should not let this matter rest on the shoulders of Glouwo alone. I pledge six of our best trackers to hunt down Werito and his demon companion."

The elders mumbled. "But Rigjo, the herds are on the move. We don't think it is wise to send so many to return a weak shaman and a calf."

Rigjo lifted his hand and silenced the room. "This is no ordinary calf. I had a vision last night. The demon spawn possesses great power. If he is not killed, he will slay many Rigjos with his black heart."

Anku stood. His old tired legs wobbled before steadying himself. "I had a similar dream many months ago. If he is allowed to live, he will lead the naked ones against us in war. Fitted with their metal skins and teeth, he conquers all of Kerisis and delivers us into slavery."

The crowd gasped in horror. Kridja thought she might pee on the dirt floor of the hut. Was Kaph punishing her for infidelity? But, how could she have denied the Rigjo?

Elder Iska growled. He stood violently and slammed his staff down on the hard word under the Elder table. "This cannot pass! The elders pledge ALL hunters to bringing the spawn back and we order the death of Werito for crimes against Kerisis!

Rigjo nodded. "Let it be done!"

***

Swila trudged through the sloppy salt flat mud and ran her hand over her empty knife sheath. She hoped her father wouldn't notice. Surely he would yell at her and give her extra chores, but it was worth it to help a friend. Besides, she was becoming a woman. It was time he allow her to live with her mistakes. She climbed up a slippery gray mud ridge and saw most horrendous thing she had ever seen. It was the size of a crocodile, but had many spindly insect-like legs. The beast had two long giant pinchers and quills along its back The monster had a leash around its neck that was being led by a large minotaur. He had a long spear with a rock chip tip. His fur was jet black though somewhat mottle with gray mud.

Swila slowly ducked down on the other side of the ridge and climbed down as fast as she could. Terror ripped through her. She splashed into the small pool and trudged through the waist deep water. She could hear the command of the minotaur. He urged the beast forward. Swila merged from the pool and glanced behind her. The monster had peaked the ridge. How could she out run them? She shrieked as she ran. Her legs felt heavy and slow. Swila could hear the monster's jaws clicking and popping as it drew near. Pain ripped through her leg as the beast caught her from behind. She toppled forward into the hot mud. The monster leapt on her back. She closed her eyes tight and prayed her death was swift.

***

"Don't kill it, Morwen." Glouwo commanded. "It's likely a scout for the others."

Swila lay motionless. She could feel warm sticky blood dripping from her leg. She wasn't sure if it was still there. She couldn't feel her feet or wiggle her toes. Who were the others? Was there a patrol from her village? She prayed to Stephanis it was so.

"Flip it over."

The Morwen roughly took Swila in its jaws and turned her. She shrieked. "I don't mean any harm. I'm friends with Blarik."

Glouwo wasn't sure what he was more surprised about. The fact that the naked body spoke his tongue or that she claimed to know the demon spawn. "How do you know him? Where are the others?"

"What others?"

"Did the rest of your party kidnap the white calf?"

"You mean Blarik?" She tried not to look at the hideous Morwen in face.

Glouwo rammed the butt end of his spear into Swila's shoulder. She cried out in pain. "Yes, you stupid naked one. Tell me where he is or I will kill you."

Swila cried. She couldn't feel her leg. It was probably severely injured. The minotaur had surely broke a few ribs and maybe her shoulder when he hit her. Clearly he was going to kill her. He would probably kill Blarik too. If he cared for him, he wouldn't have treated one of his friends like this. "Blaro, run!" she screamed before she turned her head and waited for the killing blow.

Glouwo glanced around him. Why did she yell that? Was the boy nearby? "Blarik!" he shouted. "It's Da."

Glouwo's voice echoed across the salt flats. He turned to Swila. "Call to him."

Swila felt tears well up in her eyes. She knew he had no interest in finding Blarik. He intended to kill him. "Blarik, run! He will kill you!"

Glouwo narrowed his eye. "You little bitch."

"Burn in hell!" Swila spat at the huge minotaur.

Glouwo rammed his spear into Swila's belly. The sharp stone tip easily pierced her small body and erupted out the other side, pinning her to the mud.

Swila screamed in pain. Her hands clutched the spear. She tried to kick her legs and fight, but she could not move. Blood dripped from the corner of her mouth and she fought to remain conscious. Her arms went weak and she started getting cold. Swila cried as all went black. "Blaro, I'll miss you."

***

Werito heard the screams. It sounded like minotaur, but it clearly wasn't a minotaur voice. The old shaman scrambled up the rocks. Had his son gotten to Blarik before he could?

The old bull trudged through the thick gray mud and over a small ridge. On the other side lay a human girl, maybe fifteen years old. She was unconscious and had a thick round wound in her belly and her leg was torn to the bone. Werito navigated down the muddy slope using his gnarled old staff and knelt before the girl. Minotaur tracks littered the area, but there was another kind of tracks too.

Werito pulled out some old dried leaves from his medicine pouch. He closed his eyes and chanted a few words while crumbling the leaves in his hand. When he finished, he sprinkled the crushed leave bits over the tracks. The powder sparkled and took shape. He could see the girl attacked by a Morwen. The very image of the foul unnatural creature angered the old bull. Only his stupid son would resort to contracting with Anku. He put aside his disgust and kept watching. He saw the scene play out. Somehow this girl could speak their language and she knew Blarik.

Werito glanced to the south. Should he rush and try to intercept Glouwo? Or should he revive this girl? She may know Blarik's whereabouts. Werito placed his hand on the girl. She was cool to the touch. He closed his eyes and channeled. Warm magical energies swirled inside of him and surged through his hand into the girl. Her flesh began to mend and regain color. The wound in her belly closed and a few minutes later she opened her eyes.

"Blarik" she said weakly.

Werito smiled. He had made the right choice. "What is your name child?"

Swila struggled to focus her eyes. The voice was old, but soothing. "We have to get to Blarik. The black minotaur's hunting him with some sort of monster."

Werito placed his hand on her chest and held her down. "Yes, we will get to him. But you need to lie still for a few minutes more. Once the magic has healed your insides, we will be able to move."

Swila let her head fall back into the warm mud. In moments, she was feeling stronger. She saw the old minotaur in front of her, but she was not afraid. "You can torture me all you want. I won't betray Blarik."

The old bull nodded. "I noticed. I'm Blarik's grandfather. My son, Blarik's father, wishes to sacrifice Blarik to our god. I aim to put a stop to that."

Swila sat up. The wound in her belly was healed and she could feel her leg again. "The last thing I remember, the black one went south. But, that's not where Blarik is."

Werito leaned on his staff and stood. His old knees cracked and he grimaced. "So where is he?"

Swila got to her feet. She glanced at the evening sky.

"Back at camp cleaning his kill."

Werito motioned with his hand. "Lead the way."

Swila climbed back up the warm gray mud ridge. "It's along the river."

"That's great. I have a boat."

***

48

Blarik wiped sweat from his brow. His white fur was clumped with perspiration from working hard to clean all of the meat from the crab. He discovered that if he cooked the meat while it was still in the shell, the outside formed a sharp red color and it was less likely to char. The evening sky had slowly faded and the first stars were starting to twinkle.

Blarik gently scrapped the crabmeat from the inside of a charred shell and placed it on a flat rock he had gathered from the stream.

"Blarik?"

The young bull glanced up and squinted across his campfire into the darkness. "Da?"

Werito emerged from the shadows. He carried his hunting spear and held some odd looking monster by a thick metal leash.

Blarik stood excitedly. "Da, I know you might be mad because I ran off. But, look! I made a spear, and I killed a salt crab."

"Blarik…"

"I even cooked it for ma. Are you proud of me?"

Glouwo felt a pang of guilt. It was a shame what he had to do. "Son, we have to get back. You've done well."

Blarik felt his heart race. "You mean it? You're not mad at me?"

Glouwo glanced around the shadows in search of Werito. "No son. I'm very proud. You're proving yourself to be a mighty bull."

Blarik's heart raced. He had done it. His father loved him!

"Let's gather this up and take it home to ma."

Glouwo glanced to the west. The sun had long vanished behind the horizon. "There is little time. Gather up what you can and let's go."

The Morwen cocked his head to the north. The beast pulled on the chain. Its feelers shuffled into the air. Glouwo squinted to the north. He could see a small skiff navigating down the river. "Werito."

Blarik looked north. The warm west wind blew his sweaty hair about his face. Swila poked her head out from over the bulwark. "Swila?"

"Stand back, boy. The old man shouldn't be here." Glouwo tightened his grip on his spear.

***

"Be ready, Swila. When we get close, I'm going to leap out. I want you get to Blarik into the boat." Werito tightened his grip on his staff; his son was an able warrior.

Swila nodded. She wasn't sure what she had stumbled into. This old minotaur wasn't exactly forth coming, but clearly the black bull was not a friend. She poked her head above the edge of the boat. She could see the monster, Glouwo. He stood at the edge of the river. His dark black fur shimmered in the twilight. Blarik stood behind him. She smiled. He had cut up a most of the crabmeat and cooked it.

Werito steered the skiff to the bank, just a few dozen yards from Glouwo. He clumsily slid over the side into the shallow water. Swila ducked back down.

Werito took a deep breath. "I won't let you kill the boy."

Glouwo lifted his spear from the riverbank. "This is none of your business, old bull. The tribe has spoken."

"What do you mean, da? You said you were proud of me."

Glouwo ignored Blarik. "Last chance, old bull. Get back in your boat and go back to village."

Werito stuck his hand in his pouch. He had one acorn for this. "You make me sad, son. So be it."

Glouwo released the chain on the Morwen. "Kill him!"

The Morwen turned and bounded toward the water. "Get the bull, you stupid monster!"

Werito lowered his staff. Green energy swirled around the tip. "Uro!"

The grass around Glouwo snaked up his legs and held him. The Morwen splashed into the river and swam toward the boat.

Swila popped over the side. "Blarik, get in the boat! Hurry!"

Blarik grabbed up a small cache of crabmeat and ran for the boat. Swila took his arm to help him hop in.

"That spider monster is getting close." Blarik ran to the back of the boat. The beast was leaving a wake as it closed on them.

Glouwo ripped through the weak grass and charged Werito. "Your tribe betrayal ends tonight!"

Werito wrestled with what to do. He had one thunder seed. He could use it on Glouwo, or he could save the boy from the Morwen. Werito clenched his fist around the acorn. He rocketed his arm forward and sent the seed hurling through the air. Even as Glouwo's spear pierced his body, Werito watched the thunder seed's arched descent.

Glouwo growled and punched Werito in the face. The old bull fell to the grassy earth and blood poured from his wound. Glouwo climbed atop of Werito. He wrenched the spear and revealed in the old bull's pain. He pulled a sharpened antler from his boot and pressed it against his father's neck. "You're stupid old man. Where is your shaman powers now?"

A thunderous boom answered. Glouwo turned to see bright red bits of blood and gore falling from the sky. Werito smiled weakly. "May the shark god embrace you in his maw."

"You'll see him first!" Glouwo stabbed the antler into Werito's throat. The wounded old bull gurgled briefly and died.

***

Swila grabbed the edge of the skiff. She could see the monster getting closer. "Blarik, do you have my dagger?"

Blarik pulled the sharpened steel and ran to the edge of the boat. It listed a little under his weight. He steadied himself and took aim. He had only one throw at this.

As he was about to throw, a massive blast erupted in front of him. The blast splintered the side of the boat and knocked the pair to their backs. The sound was deafening. Blarik struggled to get to his knees. He wasn't sure where the knife went. He was dizzy and it felt like the boat was spiraling in circles. He couldn't hear anything other than a sharp ringing in his ears. Bits of blood and gore splattered in the boat. Pieces of the still twitching Morwen quivered next to him. Blarik crawled over to Swila. She was on her back and unconscious, but she was breathing. He struggled to get to his feet. Blarik leaned over the edge of the boat. The

51

steady current was increasing the distance between he and his father. He could see Werito's lifeless spear pierced body on the bank of the river.

Blarik's blue eyes filled with tears. He waved goodbye to his father. He knew the bull had tried to kill him, but Blarik couldn't shake the sadness of sailing away. He may have been wicked, but he was still the only father he had. Blarik slinked down inside the boat. The entire south section was gone. Water lapped up over what was left of the bulwark. Blarik gently lifted Swila to the forecastle. Their combined weight lifted the damaged aft end from the water. He cradled her head. She was his only family now.

A SEA OF DESPAIR

Blarik leaned back against the rail of the damaged skiff. The evening sky had all but washed away revealing the twinkling starscape. He couldn't see the shoreline anymore and he wondered how long they had been adrift. The ocean was so vast; it was starting to scare him. He couldn't wake Swila. He used her knapsack to prop up her head and he frequently dabbed her head with a wet rag. She didn't feel cold to him but he covered her legs with her bed roll. He knew when he didn't feel well he would slide his rug over his legs and it kept him from being too hot or too cold.

A small gull landed on the bow of the skiff. It was large for a bird. Its feathers were brilliant white and its wings hung down as it panted.

"You tired?" Blarik felt silly talking to the bird.

The gull cocked its head to the side nervously.

"I can't see the shore anymore, so you must have really flown a long ways."

The gull scooted to the edge of bow and kept a wary eye on the white minotaur.

Blarik picked at the splinter edge of the rail, occasionally glancing back to check on Swila.

Hours passed and the twilight sky transitioned into night. The stars were in full bloom and the moon cast down a heavenly glow on the water. Blarik liked how the reflection of the moonlight seemed to form a path. The young bull placed his head down on the rail and soon was fast asleep.

***

"How much further, Mr. Tibbs?"

The squat gnome climbed atop the rail of the fast frigate. He gripped the line rigging and pulled himself up. Waves crashed against the side of the ship and the heavy sails creaked from the strong early morning winds. "I don't see them anymore for the second day, Captain. I'd say we ditched 'em fer good."

Captain Tarrar wiped his hands on his face careful not to get them into his tar filled hair. "Helmsman, come to course two-six-five."

"Two-six-five, aye sir."

The ship slowly listed to the starboard. Riggers hustled to shift sails and rotate the booms. Steady wave crests turned into a rhythmic pounding as the Undaunted cut through the water.

A whistle sounded from the crow's nest. Tibbs leaned out over the side as the watch made a signal.

"What is it Mr. Tibbs?" Captain Tarrar moved to the fantail railing above the quarterdeck. "What does he see?" Tibbs hoped down from the rail and moved to the bottom of the steps. "Says he sees a marooned skiff a mile off of our port side."

"Bearing?"

Tibbs signaled back up to the crow's nest. The watch looked through his spyglass again and signaled back.

"He says about two-four-five relative bearing, Captain."

Captain Tarrar placed his hands behind his back and pursed his lips. "What do you say, Mr. Tibbs? See what we can salvage from the skiff or keep putting time between us and that naval vessel?"

The gnome tapped his stubby fingers on the wooden bulwark. "Well captain, I don't think they will catch us anytime soon."

"Agreed. Helmsman, report."

"Passing one-nine-zero."

"Steady on course two-zero-zero and belay your headings."

"Two-zero-zero, aye sir."

The captain moved down the stairs and stood next to Tibbs. Both stared off the port side to see the skiff as it came into view. "What do you think we will find, Mr. Tibbs?"

Tibbs thumbed the hand axes that hung from either side of his belt. "Hopefully a runaway gold transfer."

The captain chuckled. "Wouldn't that be grand? I'd love to see it."

"As you should, Captain."

***

Blarik awoke to the distant sounds of waves crashing. He rubbed his tired eyes and checked on Swila. She was still unconscious. Blarik picked at the dried blood coming from her ears. He knew that probably wasn't very good. He stroked her hair gently. It was so fine compared the hair of his people, much like his own super fine hair. His mother had often mocked him for it.

The waves cresting got louder. Blarik climbed to the edge of the bulwark and peered over. The most amazing thing he had ever seen approached him. It was some sort of skiff, but it was the largest thing Blarik had seen. It had giant sails all over it, some the size of trees. There seemed to be three main masts, as opposed to his small skiff's one. The ship blasted through the ocean at great speeds.

"Swila, I wish you could see this. It's so neat." Blarik glanced over in hopes his only friend had awakened. He placed both hands on the skiff and lowered himself down so just his eyes peered over. The closer the ship got, the less inspiring it became. As it neared a hundred yards, the vessel was quite terrifying.

***

"What do you see, Mr. Tibbs?" Captain Tarrar fidgeted with his hat.

Tibbs leaned precariously over the side of the quarterdeck. One hand grasped the heavy line rigging while the other shielded his eyes from the sun. He peered down into the damaged skiff. "You're not going to believe this one Captain."

"It can't be that bad, Mr. Tibbs."

"It appears to be a small white minotaur."

Captain Tarrar sighed. "Those savages hardly ever have any loot. Though, a white one might fetch some good prices at market."

"There is worse news, Captain."

"Oh?"

"It appears to have captured a woman for dinner."

Captain Tarrar gasped. "Perhaps we should sail onward? Leave the monster to his feast."

Tibbs shook his head. "Surely a dilemma, Captain. I mean, if we leave one of yer own to the monster, surely that will not sit well with the men. If we kill the monster, we lose any chance of making any money from the haul."

The captain rubbed his chin. "Aye, Mr. Tibbs. Not to mention the trouble we would have for bringing a woman on board. Could we be lucky enough for her to be fat and displeasing to the eyes?"

Tibbs shook his head. "No sir. In fact, I would call her quite a catch for your people if you don't mind the pun, sir."

The captain pursed his lips. "Drop a grapple as we pass, Mr. Tibbs. We have slowed enough as it is."

"Sir, the minotaur will likely toss it off."

"So? If he does, we sail on. I've no time for hassles with stupid beasts."

Tibbs called for a grapple and line. One of his men handed it to him while he glanced down at the approaching skiff. "And what of the woman?"

The Captain turned his back and started up the stairs to the helm. "She is no concern to us, Mr. Tibbs. We are pirates, not heroes. Let the gods send her some other white knight."

***

56

Blarik gazed up at the huge ship as it came alongside his skiff. The mere enormity of the thing was daunting. It was easily over a hundred feet long. Fresh splintered wood spotted the side like it had been damaged recently. Swila's people scattered the decks, including one really small squat looking one that hung out over the rail. He dangled precariously over the water and carried a rope with a claw on the end. It looked like it was made of the same material as Swila's knife. The squat fellow stuck out his tongue and swung the claw back and forth before letting it go. The heavy hook landed in the skiff with a thud. Blarik quickly moved away from it and loomed over Swila. He wasn't sure how he could protect her, but he would do his best.

The giant ship sailed past forcing the line to go taught. The claw hook came to life. If skittered and bounced across the deck of the small skiff and wedged itself under the bow. The skiff lurched into life, knocking Blarik from his feet. He got to his feet and checked Swila as his skiff rocketed through the water alongside the huge vessel.

***

"It's hooked, Captain."

"Good show, Mr. Tibbs. Now, reel it in and send down a boarding party to search it and recover the woman."

"What of the minotaur?"

"Place him in irons and take him below."

"Aye, sir." Tibbs dropped a rope ladder over the side. It landed in the skiff.

"You can take some help with you if you like, Mr. Tibbs."

The gnome grinned wickedly as he lowered himself over the edge. "No, sir. I'm more than capable of handling that little thing."

Several sailors watched Tibbs descend down into the skiff. They lowered a body harness after him.

Tibbs paused at the edge of the rope ladder and glanced behind him. The minotaur showed no outward signs of aggression. In fact, he seemed protective of the girl. Tibbs dropped down into the boat. "You speak common tongue?"

Blarik felt his heart race. He wasn't sure what this human child wanted with him or Swila. "What do you want?"

The sailors laughed. "I think he is mooing at you, Tibbsy!"

Tibbs shot them an angry glare before turning back to Blarik. The boy didn't seem to be armed. He wore a small loin cloth that had woven thread in it. Two things uncommon with minotaur culture. "Captain…"

Captain Tarrar leaned over the edge of the fantail. "Yes, Mr. Tibbs? Why are you not done yet?"

"Captain, the minotaur is wearing a loin cloth most likely made by human hands. I suspect he is protecting the girl, not planning to eat her."

"Good grief." The Captain rubbed his chin. "I don't care if has eaten half of her already, Mr. Tibbs. Get them on board or you'll find yerself in the galley scrubbing pots and pans the rest of the week."

Tibbs moved slowly toward the minotaur. He pulled out a pair of manacles. He figured the boy to be an easy mark, but he hadn't lived as long as he had by being reckless.

Blarik watched the child approach. He didn't look like a child in the face. Maybe he was just a really small human. He carried two bracelets that were connected in the middle with a chain. They were not very decorative compared to the fine vessel the small human sailed on. Blarik pointed to Swila and stepped back. He couldn't speak her language, but maybe would be able to help her.

Tibbs watched in surprise as the minotaur motioned to the girl. She had taken a nasty blow to the head. Blood had dried in her ears and she likely would die soon. He looped the body harness under her arms and motioned back to the ship. "Get her to Jenison. Have him see about healing her."

Blarik watched her get hauled up. He stepped toward the edge of the skiff to be hauled up as well. The short man placed one of the bracelets on his wrist but it wouldn't fit. The metal pinched his arm and Blarik jerked back.

The minotaur was resisting. Tibbs rocketed into combat.

The short man kicked Blarik in the shin and pinched him in the meat on the side of his thigh right above his knee. Blarik felt his hooves tingle and a shooting pain erupt his leg. These were not nice men.

Tibbs was astounded; not only did the beast take a kick to shins with his steel clodhoppers on, he shrugged off the punch to the thigh. This monster was surely going to be a good romp.

Blarik stepped back. "Stay away from me, or I will defend myself."

Tibbs stepped forward. Blarik struck out, but the agile gnome ducked under it and delivered a second blow to Blarik's thigh. His foot went numb and he stumbled to backward. The human was remarkably quick.

Blarik punched again. This time, the gnome deflected his punch and twisted his arm around forcing him to face the deck of the ship. Pain erupted in his elbow and shoulder and he could feel his wrists being tied behind his back. He struggled to get free, but the bounds held him fast.

Tibbs slid the harness under his shoulders and gave the signal. Blarik watched as he was pulled into the air away from the skiff. The small man climbed back onto the rope ladder and loosed his grandfather's boat. It slowly drifted away.

Blarik was hauled onto the quarterdeck. He ignored the angry shouts and the words he didn't understand and instead gazed at the marvelous floating creation. There were ropes everywhere, and DD shaped devices that the ropes were fed into. There were wooden tents placed on the boat, odd looking spiked levers, nets, and other assorted things. Blarik stole as many images as he could before they took him below. It was like an instant transformation into another world. It was dark and the air was filled with heavy smells like a medicine man's tent. Odd giant metal shaped cylinders sat on wooden boxes and lined the walls on both sides.

Before Blarik could take all the sights in from this level, he was hauled down again. This place was darker than the other one. The air was even heavier and reeked of feces and body odor. Dozens of off looking monsters were kept in rooms with thick heavy bars in front of them. Blarik was tossed into a small room as well. They closed a barred door. They were saying things he could not understand. One of them punched Blarik in the face and spit on him. He fell to his side in the dirty cage and watched the men scamper back up the stairs that they came from. Blarik let his head fall to the cool damp wooden floor.

He knew he would never see home again. The thoughts of watching his da kill his grandfather replayed over in his mind. Blarik cried. He missed his mother. He sobbed for several minutes before falling asleep on the cold hard salty wooden deck of his cell.

Blarik opened his weary eyes. Several men stood outside of his cell. They were talking amongst themselves. The squat little gnome was there too, the one that captured him.

"I don't know Mr. Tibbs, he doesn't look very menacing to me." A sailor said doubtfully.

Tibbs shrugged, "Well, we will never know unless we test him. Captain wants to know if he can be sold to the pits when we hit the south coast."

"What are we going to use? We don't have any predators onboard for him to fight."

Tibbs folded his thick arms under his chest. "What about the mutinous dog, Hornel? The captain might approve putting him against the minotaur. No loss if he dies. The captain was planning on keel hauling him anyway."

The crew member chuckled. "Hornel? He would eat that minotaur alive."

Tibbs shrugged. "Perhaps. There is only one way to find out. Go get him, Jack."

The dark scruffy haired sailor nodded and scampered up the stairs.

Tibbs leaned against the cage and kneeled. Blarik stared at him with bright blue eyes. "I think there is something about you, beast."

Blarik could not understand what the gnome was saying. He wished Swila were with him but at least she was safe with her people.

"I want you to fight."

Blarik couldn't tell what the gnome was trying to tell him, but he was clearly saying something important. Blarik leaned in closer.

Tibbs felt his nerves go on edge. The very sight of the boy monster was intimidating. "Boy, you need to fight soon. You need to live. There is something about you, but I'm not sure what it is yet." Tibbs made fists and held them up in front of Blarik and motioned like he was punching.

Blarik frowned. The little man was making fighting motions. What did he mean? Blarik mimicked him. The gnome smiled and nodded. Blarik wasn't sure what he meant, but clearly he had communicated something to him.

"I think he will be fine. Get that scurvy scum down here." Tibbs commanded.

Blarik watched as the others pulled a man down the stairs. His arms were bound and he clearly looked like a prisoner. He began to worry about Swila. What had they done with her?

"Where's Swila?"

The men laughed. "It speaks."

Another pointed. "I wonder what he said."

"I think he said he's horny and wants to make Hornel its new woman!" The men laughed.

Hornel squirmed. "What are you going to do with me?"

Tibbs walked up to the prisoner. His head barely came up to the man's thigh, but Hornel was clearly afraid of the menacing gnome. "You got one chance, Hornel. You kill the minotaur, and we will set you free at the next port."

Hornel looked into the cage doubtfully. The beast was about the size of a man, but it looked anything but fierce. "Like, I'm to believe you. Win or not, you will surely keel haul me."

"Be that as it may, I guess you can choose to die today or take a chance at being released later."

Hornel nodded. "Do I get a blade?"

Tibbs shook his head. "No, it's you versus the beast. It's going to take a while, for sure."

"So, I am for sport?"

Tibbs was starting to get frustrated. "No, fool. The gods have been on us enough as it is. We don't want to kill either of you without a sporting chance. So, this fight eliminated two problems for us."

Hornel glanced at the cage. "And what if the minotaur wins?"

Tibbs smiled. "Well, rest assured that's one problem you'll not be burdened with." The men laughed.

"Okay, you Nancys, spread out. Give these two some room." Tibbs shouted. "I want four at each ladder well. No one escapes to the upper decks. If they try, run them through." "Man or beast?" One man asked.

"Aye, man or beast."

The sailors fumbled with Hornel's manacles and Tibbs went to Blarik's cage. "Okay, boy." he waved his fists again. "It's time. You or him."

Blarik watched the events unfold with confusion. The men were clearly guarding the stairs, but they were releasing the prisoner. He was even more shocked when the gnome opened his cage. The red haired man moved around the edge of the other men like he was stalking him. It dawned on Blarik he was to fight this man. "I don't want to fight anyone. I'm only a hunter."

The men all laughed. "He is singing to you, Hornel. He is going to violate your arse!"

Hornel charged in. Blarik steady himself. He really didn't know how to fight. He punched out, but the man ducked under and rammed his shoulder into Blarik's chest. The force of the blow knocked the air from Blarik and the slippery deck slid out from under his hooves. The floor greeted him hard. He fought for breath and the man slid on top of him. He could feel the man's legs slide under his hips. Blarik tried to get up when the man struck him in the face. He saw a flash of light and his nose stung. He instinctively stuck his arms up but his watery eyes made his vision cloudy as blow after blow came down.

His face went numb as the man hit him time and time again.

"Hornel is kicking its ass!"

"Fight back, fool." Tibbs shouted. Blarik covered his head and looked toward the voice of the gnome. He could vaguely see the little man making the punching motions with his hands. But how was he going to fight? The red haired man was on top of him and had him pinned to the ground.

Hornel began to heave from exertion. He shook his right hand and punched with his left. When he was finished shaking out his sore knuckles, he switched and started punching with the other hand.

"The stupid cow won't fight."

Tibbs slumped his shoulders. He thought he had conveyed what the boy needed to do.

Blarik could tell that Tibbs was frustrated with him. His dad always gave him the same look. Blarik thought of his parents. They used to beat him like this, but they hit much harder and they did it much more savagely. Blarik thought about his father killing his grandfather. Maybe he should just let the red haired human kill him. His father hated him, his mother hated him, and he was a disgrace to his tribe. What was there to live for?

Hornel wiped sweat from his brow and struck Blarik with a heavy elbow. The force of the blow split the skin under Blarik's eye. Coppery blood dripped out and soaked his bright white fur.

"First blood!" A sailor shouted.

Blarik felt himself fall into a despair like when his parents beat him. He used to take his mind to a faraway place. He would think of the times he got to spend with Swila. Swila. The name seemed to rip Blarik from his seclusion. He felt a rage from deep inside of him. Had they done this to Swila? She would never let these men do this to him if she was alive. Was she dead?

Another blow struck the boy in the face. The sound echoed in his mind and awakened something feral. Blarik turned his head and stared at the red haired man from underneath. His soft blue eyes narrowed and his brow creased with rage. Hornel dropped another elbow. Blarik accepted the blow and wrapped his thick arms around the back of Hornel's neck and pulled him close. He opened his mouth and bit down on the inside of Hornel's arm. The man shrieked in pain. Blarik maintained his bite against the flailing man. He could feel the flesh beginning to tear away. With Hornel trying to get up, Blarik pushed, knocking the man to the side. He stood up and snarled. He felt a new emotion, hatred. "Where is Swila?"

The men standing around flinched. "Tibbs, watch out. The monster is losing it."

Tibbs pointed to Hornel. Blarik was not sure what he was meaning. Was he suggesting that the red haired man had done something to Swila?

Hornel grasped the bite wound on his arm. He could hardly lift it; the monster had bitten clean through his bicep.

"Give me a blade!"

"No blades!" Tibbs shouted.

Blood streamed down Hornel's arm and made a steady drip from his hand. He turned and pleaded to the crowd. "A dirk, can't you just give me a dirk? He has teeth, I have nothing."

Blarik watched as one of the men started to pull a knife. He remembered how sharp Swila's knife was. If that man got a knife, Blarik knew he would probably die. Blarik's thick powerful legs flexed and he charged forward. His heavy hoof falls cladded across the deck. Blarik lowered his head and horns and rammed into Hornel just as he grasped the dirk. Blarik felt the man's bones snap from the force of the blow. Hornel was hurled through the air and collided with the men standing around. They force knocked them all the ground. Blarik didn't miss a step. He strode over the Hornel and the other sailors scurried away from the white beast. The wounded sailor turned to his back and glanced up. Blood poured from his mouth. He gasped and choked.

"Where's Swila?" Blarik growled.

The sailors started to pull their blades.

"Hold your blades!" Tibbs commanded.

Hornel didn't answer. He started to roll to his side and reach for the dirk that lay on the deck next to him. Blarik growled and slammed his heavy hoofed foot down on Hornel's head. The man's thin skull collapsed under the force of the stomp. Blood and pink matter squirted across the deck.

"Holy fuck!" One of the sailors cried out as the others looked to Tibbs.

Tibbs slowly started toward the minotaur with his hands up in front of him. "Okay, boy, well done."

Blarik turned and regarded the crowd. "Where is Swila?"

"Swila?" Tibbs asked, repeating the world Blarik kept using.

Blarik relaxed. His feral raged drained. "Yes, where is she?"

Tibbs shook his head. "I don't know what you are saying. What's a Swila?"

Blarik growled in frustration.

"Maybe he means the girl?" One of the sailor's asked.

Tibbs nodded. "Bring me some leg irons."

"I don't think they will fit him, Mr. Tibbs."

Tibbs shot the man a glare. "They are for his wrists. Now get yer arse up the deck and get me some fucking irons."

The sailor nodded and scurried up the stairs. Tibbs turned back to Blarik. He pulled out a hanky from his pocket and made a wiping motion to his nose and eye before tossing the cloth to Blarik. The boy stared at the gnome for a moment before dabbing his stinging cuts. It was becoming obvious he could communicate with the gnome by making signals. He pinched his fingers together to what he guessed the size of a beetle might be. "Swila" he said again.

Tibbs was truly confused. At first he thought the boy meant the girl's name was Swila, but now it looked like he was trying to act out a bug.

Blarik frowned. He realized that they didn't speak his language so trying to explain that Swila meant beetle would be lost on them. He wiped the blood from his nose and began to motion for long hair.

Tibbs nodded. "Yep, I think he wants to see the girl."

The sailor came back down the stairs with the leg irons and handed them to Tibbs. All of the sailors kept their distance.

"Okay, boy. You need to put these on so I can take you to see yer friend."

Blarik noticed the gnome had the metal bracelets again. He appeared to be motioning that he wanted him to wear them. Blarik stuck out his arms. Tibbs gently slid the leg irons on Blarik's wrists. He locked them in place. Blarik brought the cloth back up to his face and gently dabbed his cuts.

"What are we suppose to do with, Hornel?"

Tibbs led the minotaur up the stairs. "You guys know how to sink a man. Make it happen."

"No last honors?" One sailor asked.

Tibbs shook his head as he disappeared up the stairs. "No, he was a mutinous thief. He deserves less than he got."

Tibbs was halted by one of the sailors. "Mr. Tibbs. The captain is calling for you."

Tibbs sighed. "Okay, secure him to one of the canons there. I'll be back shortly."

The sailor unlocked the manacle of one of Blarik's hands and slid it under the rocker iron of the cannon and re-secured it on his wrist. He kept a wary eye on the bloodied minotaur.

Blarik watched Tibbs disappear up the next deck. He glanced around before sitting down. There wasn't much else to do until the gnome came back.

MONSTERS AND MEN

"Blarik?" Swila opened her heavy eyes.

"I'll be damned." Jenison lightly dabbed the damp cloth on her forehead. "She speaks the minotaur's language."

Tibbs arched a skeptical eyebrow. "What makes you think she is speaking anything?"

Jenison thumbed the pearl holy symbol that hung loosely from his neck. "I don't know. Just makes sense."

"Dad?" Swila drifted back into unconsciousness.

"Is she going to live?" Tibbs was clearly annoyed. "I'm tired of being in this damn sick bay on babysitting duty."

"Time will tell. I have used all the healing spells I have, but the injury is to her mind." Tibbs groaned.

"You can go, Mr. Tibbs. There is no fear of her waking for many days."

"Thank the stars." The squat gnome opened the brass handle of the decorated sick bay door and stepped out onto the quarterdeck. The evening sun washed down over the ship and peaked through the heavy sails.

The last few days had been trying ones. The Kingston ship had been close enough to fire on them several times. They'd suffered no casualties, but the unusual thing was the ship was unknown to them. The captain suspected it was a new frigate, but normally ships went about their patrols once they had escaped. This ship seemed to have no patrol responsibilities and was able to find them time after time. It was unnatural the way the vessel seemed to track them. The crew had started to murmur to themselves of curses and damnation by the gods.

"You okay, Mr. Tibbs?"

Tibbs was roused from his contemplations by the skinny navigator, Patar. "I'm fine, Pat. Just a lot on my mind."

Patar nodded and glanced to the west. The setting sun was painting its orange stripe on the waves. "Can I speak my mind, Mr. Tibbs?"

The gnome nodded and rested his arms on the rail. "Sure."

Patar glanced around and leaned in close. "I mean no disrespect, Mr. Tibbs. But was it a smart move to bring the monster and the woman onboard?"

Tibbs popped a half smile. "I think you are missing the other question, Pat."

Patar frowned and picked at his teeth a moment. "The other question?"

"Yes, the other question. Why do you fear picking them up?"

Patar shrugged. "That doesn't really seem like a side question, Mr. Tibbs."

"That isn't the other question, Pat. But, I'm getting to it."

"Oh, I see. Okay okay, well. It's bad luck to bring a woman on board. And with that ghost ship's knack to find us in open waters, I think we need all the luck we can get."

Tibbs nodded. "So, it would seem that Surshy has left us to the shark god, right?" Patar nodded.

"So, then why would we turn our backs on the other gods and condemn a woman to die alone at the hands of a vicious monster in the middle of the ocean?"

"So yer saying that we could have earned some favor from one of the other gods by saving the woman?"

Tibbs scratched his head. "Something like that."

Patar smiled, clearly relieved. "Thanks, Mr. Tibbs."

Tibbs stared off at the setting sun. He hoped the winds would pick up and get them to port. The sooner they were able to escape that frigate the better.

"The captain will see you now, Mr. Tibbs."

Tibbs nodded at the sailor made his way aft to the Captain's quarters. He knocked on the door once.

"Come in, Mr. Tibbs."

Tibbs turned the brass handled and walked in. The quarters were as lavish as any duke's chamber. There were water charts, star charts, and other relics from past conquest adorning the walls. The heavy polished oak tables and chairs were fixed to the floor and the crystal chandelier that hung from the ceiling was secured with an iron rod, keeping it from being jostled around in heavy seas.

"So, I hear you dealt with Hornel."

Tibbs nodded. "Aye, Captain. And I believe I did it in such a way as to appease the gods that set the boy in our path." "The boy?"

Tibbs nodded. "Aye, sir. He is clearly a youth of his people."

The captain procured a small wooden box from his desk. He flipped the lid and pulled out a thick brown cigar. "Would you like a smoke, Mr. Tibbs?"

Tibbs shook his head. "No thank you, sir. No time to enjoy it. I have the boy secured to a cannon and do not wish to dally."

Captain Tarrar clipped the end of the cigar and let it fall back into the box. "And why is the monster secured to one of my guns?"

"I plan to take him to see the girl."

The captain struck a long match and let if flair for a few seconds before allowing it burn down to light his smoke. He puffed a few times. Thick smoke tendrils collected around his face. He squinted from the smoke and leaned back in his chair. "So why are we going to reunite the beauty with the beast?"

"I think them friends. Not captor and captive."

"And what is to be gained from this?"

Tibbs pursed his lips. "Permission to speak freely, sir?"

The captain took a long draw from his cigar. "Mr. Tibbs, we have been friends for many years. Tell me what's on that brilliant mind of yours."

"What if we didn't sell him to the pits, captain? What if we made him a pirate?"

The captain coughed and laughed. He sat up from his chair. "Have you been set upon by sun sickness, Mr. Tibbs?"

"Think about, sir. He crushed Hornel and he is just a boy right now. Imagine what a great asset he could be to the ship when he's grown?"

"And how will we control such a monster? If he gets as big as the stories say, how will we use him?"

Tibbs smiled. "The same way we would any child. We instill in him a solid sense of right and wrong. I suspect he is about the equivalent to a fifteen-year-old human child. Now is the time to guide him."

The captain puffed several more times. "Okay, Mr. Tibbs. You can take the boy under your watch. But, be reminded his leash is short."

"Aye Captain. Your wisdom has just strengthened this ship for years to come."

The captain smiled and popped the cork on a bottle of wine. "Time is the measure of all decisions, Mr. Tibbs. I just happen to listen to those I trust."

Tibbs nodded. "As you should."

***

Blarik sat with his legs crossed and his back against the bulkhead as he watched the gnome come back down the stairs. The gnome smiled and unlocked one of his wrists. Blarik slid his arm out and stuck it out for Tibbs to shackle again. Tibbs paused and then unshackled the other wrist. "If you fight with us, you will be killed. I'll take you to Swila."

Blarik's heart raced when he heard the gnome say her name. "Yes, Swila. Take me to her, please."

Tibbs motioned for Blarik to follow. The minotaur marveled at every feature of the ship, and now he could finally take it all in. When he crested the quarterdeck, he shielded his eyes from the sun.

Tibbs led him across the deck to the rear of the ship. He could feel the eyes of the crew staring at him, but he was too busy soaking in the sights and smells. The sounds of the sails as they creaked against the thick lines that held them against the wind sounded like a soft frequent drum. He enjoyed the moan of the wood as light seas flexed the boards in and out. The sea had a salty smell, much like the salt flats, but not as strong. And the wind, Blarik loved how the warm wind felt against his face.

Tibbs led Blarik into a small room. It was like the rooms he had back in his tribe, but the huts were made of wood. Blarik saw Swila lying on the bed. He rushed to her and kneeled beside the bed. "Swila, can you hear me?"

She jostled slightly in her sleep. "Blaro?"

Blarik stroked her cheek, much to the surprise of those in the room. "I'm here, Swila. We are safe on this ship."

Jenison placed his hands on his hips. "Surshy damn us all, she speaks his tongue."

Swila reached out and placed her hand on Blarik's cheek. "I'll be okay, Blaro. You just sit tight. We're safe now."

Blarik placed his head against her hand as she slipped back into unconsciousness. The smell of her skin made his heart hurt. She was his only family now.

Tibbs nodded. "Yep, that settles it. The white bull is here to stay."

Jenison dabbed a cool damp cloth on Swila's head. "So what did the captain say?"

Tibbs stuck his hands in his pockets. "He said the bull is under my charge. So it looks like I have my hands full the next few weeks turning this thing into a sailor."

"Mr. Tibbs." Jenison said doubtfully. "Why do we want this thing on our ship?"

"There are a million reasons I could choose, Jenison. But, the most prevalent one would be his ability to discourage boarders."

Jenison arched an eyebrow. "And I suppose the key to his training, is this girl."

Tibbs nodded. He placed his hand under Blarik's arm and motioned for him to stand. "It would seem so, Jenison."

Blarik reluctantly stood. He looked to Tibbs. "We should let her rest."

Tibbs chuckled. "Ole boy, I have no idea what the hell you are saying, but we are going to work on that first."

Blarik followed the gnome out onto the quarterdeck. The crew looked at him cautiously, but said nothing. He felt just like he did the few times he went to his village. They all pointed and whispered. Most scoffed and some even spit at him. Least, there did not seem to be any rocks on the ship.

The gnome pointed to the floor. "Deck"

Blarik nodded. "Deck."

Tibbs smiled. "Good."

Blarik nodded. Odd that he called a smile good. Learning this language was going to be hard. Tibbs took him around the ship, from forecastle to fantail. Blarik thought his name was cute. Such a pleasant name for the spit fire little man. Tibbs pointed out things that would hurt. He called it danger. At first, Blarik thought that the name of the rigging, but after a while it became apparent that these areas could pose a threat to him. There were a lot of them. Blarik wondered if there was an occurrence that a sailor had been killed from being in the wrong place at the wrong time. Tibbs took him to the fantail and pointed to the stars that were beginning to emerge from the blackening night sky. The air turned cool and the warm ocean breeze brought new smells to his nose.

"I think you have a fair grasp of where not to be, Blarik."

Blarik smiled. He had no clue what Tibbs had said, but he recognized his name.

"Swila would like this."

Tibbs looked up at the bull's face. He seemed unable to smile, but he sure could frown. His voice sounded melancholy and sad. "She'll be okay, Blarik." Tibbs placed a comforting hand on Blarik's forearm.

The young bull glanced down. The gnomes touch felt good. It was friendly. His mother or father never touched him like that. This little gnome had made him feel more at home than he ever felt with his own people. Blarik stared off into the distant sea. The ocean breeze tickled his fine white fur. He gazed into the vastness of the ocean. It was odd, how something so vast and so lifeless, seemed so warm and inviting. As long as Swila survived, life would be okayokay.

MASTERS AND COMMANDERS

"Up and at 'em, bull boy." Tibbs kicked Blarik's feet. "Someone wants to see you."

Blarik sat up from his cell. Bits of straw hung awkwardly from his fur. They had filled his cell with straw and given him a blanket. The gnome had the door taken off and it seemed like they were not interested in caging him anymore. He figured it was because they didn't believe him to be a threat. Blarik chuckled to himself and got up. He brushed the straw from his fur and contemplated the absurdity of him being a threat to anyone. He was just a young bull, not a great warrior like his father.

Tibbs shielded his face. "Good god, man. Put on your loincloth. When we need some pikes hammered in, we'll call you."

Blarik cocked his head to the side. "What?"

Tibbs backed away and pointed to Blarik's crotch. "That thing, Blarik. Put that thing away. If I wanted to stare at a one eyed sea monster in the morning, I woulda keel hauled myself."

Blarik glanced to where the gnome was pointing and spied his loincloth that Swila had made him. "Oh yes, I forgot about your people's customs, my apologies."

Tibbs shook his head from side to side. When Blarik finished dressing, he led him topside. The ship in the morning was in stark contrast with the ship at night. Sailors were busy all over. Some were sewing netting, others repairing old sails, and some even seemed to be washing the decks. Blarik didn't quite understand that, but there was much he didn't understand.

Tibbs lead Blarik into the room where they kept Swila. He ducked low under the doorway. Swila was sitting on the edge of the bed. "Swila!" He rushed to her.

She giggled and wrapped her arms around his furry neck "Oh, Blaro, you're safe. I was so worried."

"I was worried about you. You hit your head and you were bleeding. Then this ship came, and they healed you."

Tears streamed down her face. "Oh Blaro, you did it. You convinced people that you were good."

Blarik stroked her hair and squeezed her. Her touch felt so good to him. "Of course. I'm not a monster."

Swila giggled through her tears. She broke from the embrace and kissed Blarik on the snout. The sensation of her warm lips caught him off guard. "What was that?"

Swila ignored him and looked at a confused Jenison and a smiled Tibbs. "Thank you so much for sparing my friend. He is not like his people. He would never hurt anyone."

Jenison and Tibbs shared a knowing glance. Tibbs chuckled. "Swila, all men are capable of defending themselves or those they love."

"Not Blarik. I had to rescue him from his people. They treated him awful. His dad beat him and his mom did horrible things to him."

Jenison offered Swila an apple. "How do you know these things?"

"I've known Blarik since we were young. We practically grew up together. Speaking of which…" Swila grasped Blarik's arm and squeezed, "You have been growing, Blaro."

Blarik nodded. "My knees have been aching and I have been crazy hungry lately. Seems, I can't get full."

Jenison cut in, "So you lived with his people?"

"Gods, no. I was picking flowers from my mom one afternoon, and a polecat had me treed. It was climbing up after me and Blarik heard me screaming. He scared the thing away. He and I have been friends since. I think I was about ten at the time."

"So how do you know about the way he was treated?"

Swila placed her hand on Blarik's arm and snuggled into him. "I learned his language. It was easy enough. There aren't that many words."

Blarik was confused, "What are you saying, Swila?"

"I'm telling them how we met."

"You mean the story about how you saved me from the mountain lion with your sling?"

Swila nodded. "Yea, but I'm saying you saved me."

"Why would you do that?"

"Just to make sure they respect you."

Blarik nodded. "If you think that's best, my friend."

Swila turned back to the Tibbs. "Okay, so what banner do you fly under?"

Tibbs smiled. "We fly under our own."

"So, what do you haul?"

Tibbs bit the side of his lip. "You are onboard Captain Tarrar's vessel, 'The Undaunted.'"

Swila frowned. She knew most of the frigates that delivered to New Gradenbach. The ships came once a month or so to buy lumber and trade. It sounded familiar to her. "I've heard of this ship," she lied.

Tibbs was surprised. "You have? Really?"

Swila nodded. "Yes, you guys have traded with my home on East Kerisis."

Tibbs chuckled. "Well, lady. I have heard rumors of such, but I suspect that was before my time."

Swila breathed a sigh of relief. She had thought she had heard rumors of a pirate ship named Undaunted, but she couldn't remember. She was thankful this was not one of them. "Have you had any trouble with pirates?"

Jenison laughed. "Oh no. We never have any problems with pirates."

"Good. I'm deathly afraid of them."

Tibbs chuckled. "Well, Miss Swila. Many of them are right fine chaps. Given the right circumstances, I suspect they could be quite friendly."

75

Swila frowned. That was an odd comment. She had never met a sailor that did not hate, or fear pirates.

Tibbs stepped forward. "Well, enough with the reunion. For your rescue and fare, we ask you to teach Blarik here, to speak our language."

Swila smiled. "Of course. Where are we headed?"

A fair ways from your home, I'm afraid. But, once we set port, I suspect that we could drop you and your friend back off on the return."

"I'd be in your debt. I know my parents will be worried sick from my absence."

***

"This tongue is hard." Blarik complained.

Swila smiled. Her friend was so smart. "You'll get it, Blarik."

The young bull sighed. "We have been at it a whole week."

"Not in your language, only ours."

"Okay."

Swila patted his arm. "Okay, now let's work on words that begin with the sound of my name."

"Kim?"

Swila nodded. "Okay, the leader of the boat is the ..."

Blarik thought for a bit. "Captain?"

"Good!"

Blarik growled in pleasure. "Word not hard with Kim."

Swila chuckled. "You sound dumb when you speak my language."

"Remember the day my dad came? We played in the river. That was a fun day."

Swila reflected on the terrifying day. "Blarik, you watched your grandfather get killed and you barely escaped your father killing you. How could anything from that day be good?"

Blarik stared at her with his intense blue eyes. "Well, because I was with you. Every day of my life was hard like that. That was a particularly hard day, but no time is perfect."

76

Swila nodded solemnly. If all of her people had the resilience Blarik had.

"I mean, we are stuck out here in the middle of the ocean on a strange boat with strange people but since I get to spend sun up to sun down with you, it's the greatest time of my life."

"Not for me, Blarik. I miss my family. I miss my bed, my pets. I miss my farm and my people."

"But, these are your people." Blarik gestured around him. "And I can be your family."

"No, Blarik." Swila got up from the deck and loomed over the young bull, "No you can't."

"Well, you're my family. You're the only family I have,"

Swila looked into his soft blue orbs. Something was different about Blarik lately. He was gaining in confidence. He seemed to be getting bigger by the day and he was eating enough food for three men. "Blaro, you will always be my friend. But my family loves me. They miss me and it hurts me to think they are missing me right now."

Blarik stood. His heavy hooves clopped on the wooden deck. "Well, you can leave me when you want and go back to them. I don't need my parents, or my people. So, I don't need you."

Swila watched in confusion as Blarik stormed away down the stairs to the quarterdeck.

What just happened? That was the first time Blarik had ever been mad at her, or shown any outward sign of anger.

She got up and moved to the edge of the stairs. She watched Blarik talk to Tibbs. The gnome glanced back to her and then to Blarik. He chuckled and shook his head. The two walked toward the forecastle.

"Woman troubles?"

Blarik nodded. "Yes. She no happy."

"Well, you know she won't ever love you. Not like one of her own kind."

Blarik tried to take all of the gnome's words in. He was learning common, but it was so different than his own words. "What you mean? She my family."

Tibbs walked with the minotaur along the railing of the vessel. "Blarik, I mean. …She will need to be with her own kind one day. She won't ever fit in with you all the way. And you will want to be with your kind one day too."

"One day, I want go back to her village with her."

Tibbs laughed. "That would be one hell of a short visit."

"No, I stay long time."

No, I mean… I mean they would attack you. You would have to kill them all."

Blarik pondered the gnome's words. "She say that too."

"She is wise, Blarik. I know it seems simple to you, but that's because you want it. But wanting it won't make it easy or even right."

Blarik nodded. "I think I understand. Like erwo. Neighbor has it, I want it, but taking erwo is wrong."

Tibbs thought about for a bit. He wasn't sure what the hell an erwo was, but the logic was there. "Kind of, Blarik. But here on this ship, we want you. You will always fit in."

Blarik smiled. He placed his ever-growing hand on the top of Tibb's head. "Thanks Mr. Tibbs. You true friend."

Tibbs smiled. "Now, get back to your lessons with the girl. You can't be a good sailor until you learn to speak better."

Blarik nodded and started back toward the fantail. A whistle from the top of the sail grabbed his attention. He cocked his head up and shielded his eyes from the sun.

"Come with me, boy. Hurry."

Blarik followed Tibbs in confusion. "What going?"

Tibbs led Blarik around the aft mast and up the ladder on the far side to the conning deck. The Captain was standing on the edge of the fantail. His spyglass was extended and he was looking far behind them. "I can't see them yet. Quartermaster report."

The quartermaster whistled back to the man atop of the rear mast. The man raised his spyglass and whistled a second time.

"What do whistles mean?"

Tibbs angrily motioned for Blarik to keep quiet.

"11 miles, Captain."

Tarrar slammed his spyglass shut and moved to peer over the chart that was tacked down on a wide table. "They using our wind?"

"No sir, they can't be."

"There shouldn't be any current here. Not one moving south."

Tibbs gritted his teeth. "They got a mage."

The captain nodded. "And most likely a powerful one too."

"Orders, sir?"

"Nothing pressing Mr. Tibbs. I look at the charts. It will be a few days before they crest horizon and a week or better before they are on us. Get the powder up and in the bins, and have the men get our balls ready as well."

"Aye sir."

The captain went back to the charts and ignored Blarik and Tibbs.

"We have some work to do, boy. Time to learn how to be a real sailor."

"Ship following?"

Tibbs nodded. "Aye. Been on us a few weeks. Had some light skirmishes, but we have managed to outrun them."

Blarik leaned out over the side of the ship and looked behind them. "I don't see."

"They have not crested horizon yet."

Blarik growled in frustration. The gnome spoke so fast he had a hard team keeping up. The common tongue had so many useless words, like "the." Why was there even a need for that stupid word?

"Simmer down, boy. You'll get a shot at them soon enough. But, they are a good week away."

Blarik pushed off the side and followed Tibbs. "Why do it follow?"

"We captured one of their moles, Hornel. They planted him to take over the ship and return it to the royal Navy."

Blarik was so confused. What did planted mean? What was a navy? "What Navy?"

Tibbs made his way of the small steps to the forecastle. "A Navy is a nation's army of ships."

Blarik was surprised. "Army of ships? Like this?"

Tibbs opened a large chest set against the bulwark. "Yep."

Blarik tried to wrap his mind around an army of ships. That seemed crazy powerful to him.

Tibbs pulled out a scimitar and handed it to Blarik. "Here, take this."

Blarik marveled at the blade. It was three times the size of Swila's knife. It had a polished brass guard and it felt heavy in his hands. He ran his furred thumb over the brass. He could see his reflection in it. Other than seeing his reflection in water, he had never looked on himself before. He brought his hand up to his face. He was so different than Swila, so different than everyone on the ship.

"That's the hilt." Tibbs said. "It guards your hands from an enemy's blade."

Swila stormed up the forecastle stairs. "What are you doing, Mr. Tibbs?"

The gnome looked around confused. "Me?"

"Yes you," she pointed. "Why is he holding a sword?"

"We have a ship bearing down on us. They mean to take us by force. In a week or so they will be on us. I want to make sure boy blue here can fight."

"Why would the other ship attack us? Are they pirates? We fly no banner and haul no goods. We should be safe." Swila's words trailed off as she spoke them. No banner, no goods?

Why were they at sea? A ship did not sail for free. She glanced around at the ship's company. She could see old scars of battle. The men clearly were not sailors. The truth began to wash over. This was a pirate ship. But, why wasn't she raped and murdered? Clearly men of their repute were scandalous thieves and killers.

Tibbs smiled as her voice trailed off. He turned back to Blarik. "Your hand is almost too big for that blade right now. Let alone when you get larger. I'm afraid it would be a waste to teach you swordplay."

Blarik frowned. "I strong warrior and hunter. Swila seen me kill crab."

Swila nodded absently. She was in shock at the realization they were on a pirate ship.

Tibbs nodded, "This is different than fighting crabs or the scoundrel, Hornel. Though, I give you props. You squished his head like a melon."

Swila was jerked back to reality. "What do you mean? Blarik was in a fight?"

Tibbs nodded and handed a rapier to Swila. "Aye, he and the mole had it out. I thought him to lose, but ole blue boy here, knocked 'em down and crushed his head like a bug, even grossed me out a bit."

Swila looked at Blarik, he had suffered so much in his life. "He is just a boy, Mr. Tibbs. A big boy, but a boy nonetheless."

Blarik chuckled. "I no boy, Swila. I growing into strong bull."

She was losing him. He looked at Tibbs like an older brother or father. She knew if she told him what bad men they were, she would alienate herself forever. She placed her hand on his shoulder. He was so warm to the touch and it felt like his shoulder had doubled in size in the last weeks.

Blarik placed his arm around her. "Swila, you're my best friend. But, I must grow up. I must become a strong bull.

Stronger than my father and wiser than my grandfather."

Tibbs frowned. "What did he say?"

Swila pressed closer. His fur was so warm and she felt safe in his embrace. "I know, Blaro. My heart hurts for you. I wish things were different—better."

Blarik chuckled and gestured around. "Look around us, Swila. Life is better. No more beatings, no more feeling like a reject. My parents might not have loved me, but I fit in here. The only thing that could ruin my life would be to lose you."

Swila felt a tear well up in her eye. Her nose burned and she fought the urge to wrap both arms around Blarik.

"What is he saying?" Tibbs folded his arms, frustrated.

Swila started to reply, but Blarik cut her off. "She say she happy I here to defend her. I say without her, I would leave and go own way."

Tibbs nodded and handed Blarik a pair of metal gauntlets. "Good, that's what I like to hear. That kind of relationship is what will keep you both safe while on board."

Swila took a deep breath. Did Tibbs just admit this was a pirate ship? Was he trying to tell her to stay on guard? "Thank you, Mr. Tibbs. I have noticed that this was not an ordinary ship. Yet, Blarik and I consider ourselves fortunate that you took the time to bring us aboard and make us part of your crew."

Tibbs gave Swila a wink. The girl was not as dumb as she let on. This was a good thing. "Okay, boy blue. Try fitting those things on."

Blarik tried to slide his hands into the gauntlets. They were too tight for his meaty three-fingered hands. "Too tight."

Tibbs snatched the gauntlets. "No worries. I have some smithing skill. Let me see what kind of crafting I can do.

Maybe fashion you something to fit your fighting style."

Blarik nodded. "I like that."

Tibbs closed the trunk. "Swila, get him learning the common tongue faster. He is going to need it." She nodded.

"Oh, and Swila…"

"Yes?"

"Be mindful of speaking his tongue around the other crew members. They have wild imaginations. Best that no conversation is left to their imaginations."

THE UNDAUNTED

"A thousand yards starboard side!" a spotter called out as a heavy splash erupted off the side.

Captain Tarror turned hard on the helm. The booms shifted and the ship listed. "Get Mr. Tibbs up here."

Tibbs stood with his shirt off. His thick well-muscled chest was glistening with sweat. He flexed and pushed one of the cannons up onto its tracks. "Hurry up and sponge these guns. We have about fifteen minutes."

Another shot sounded out. Its muffled boom permeated the ships bulkheads and left the gun deck in an eerie silence.

"Tibbs, Captain is calling you to the deck."

Tibbs grabbed his shirt and wiped the sweat from his forehead. "Reginald, you are mount captain until I return."

The experienced sailor nodded. "Aye, Mr. Tibbs." "Come on, boy blue. Let's go see what the Captain needs."

Blarik followed Tibbs up the stairs to the quarterdeck. It had been a week since he had started training with Tibbs. Swila had taught him the common tongue fairly well. He still had a problem with many of the words. It seemed like he was learning a new one every day. "Where is Swila?"

Tibbs bounded up the stairs two at a time and rounded the rail toward the aft conning deck. "She is prolly with the Captain."

Blarik glanced off the starboard fantail. He could see the ship even closer now. A flash of smoke from the ship's bow preceded the thunder of the shot. They heavy ball splashed just off the fantail.

"Nine hundred yards, starboard side!" The spotter yelled.

Tibbs scampered up the ladder to the conning deck. "Tibbs reporting, Captain."

Tarror looked up from the helm. He was flushed and sweating. "Good to see you Mr. Tibbs. Are our port guns ready?"

Tibbs nodded. "Aye sir. Ready. All three rotations are ready."

Blarik thought back to the small metal tracks that surrounded the guns. It made sense to him now. When one cannon fired, it would rotate back in a circle and a new one would take its place.

Another thunderous boom echoed across the open ocean followed by a splash just off of the fantail. Water shot up and covered the deck.

"Eight hundred yards, sir!"

Captain Tarrar spun the helm to port. The ship responded almost immediately.

"Hold on, Blarik." Tibbs shouted.

The ship listed to the starboard side as it turned hard to port. Booms shifted and the bow bounced as it cut through the waves.

"She is still head on, sir."

"What does that mean?" Blarik felt the wooden rail creak under the weight of his ever-growing body.

Tibbs shifted his grip to the other rail. "They ranged us with their six pounders at eight hundred yards. The captain is now turning into port to show our broad side."

The Undaunted leveled off and sped through the waves.

"Ten minutes, Mr. Tibbs. Get below and get the boarders ready. I only want the riggers on deck."

Tibbs bolted down the stairs. "Aye sir,"

Blarik followed him to the quarterdeck. Tibbs began to unlock the weapon chests. "Boarders, muster!"

Men started locking down lines and lining in up in front of Tibbs.

"Axemen." Tibbs shouted and moved to the next wooden chest. Blarik watched the men grab axes from the chest.

"Swordsmen." Tibbs called out. Different men came and grabbed cutlasses and other blades. Blarik watched as they fastened a small leather strap attached to the end of the sword around their wrists.

84

"Go below to the forward line locker. Stay there and await my command. Blarik, you come with me."

Blarik followed the gnome to a small room near the ladder to the gun deck. Blarik had seen the gnome in there working long hours. "What's line locked?"

"Line locker," Tibbs corrected. "It's where we keep all of our mooring lines. The boarders go there. It is the least strategic place to strike a ship to disable it. So it is the safest place for our men." Tibbs rummaged through bits of metal and scrap. "Ah, here it is."

"What is it?"

Tibbs handed Blarik two large metal contraptions shaped like a glove. The insides were leather and the metal plating was affixed on the outside. The left one had two long sharp claw looking appendages and the right was thick and shaped like a fist. It had large spiked studs on where his knuckles would be. "What do I do with this?"

"This is what I have been working on for you." Tibbs exhaled and ducked under Blarik's arm. He slid the odd gauntlet on his left hand and tied the plating in place that extended up to his elbow. "This one is for defending. Use those spikes to stop swords. They are strong enough even stop a club I hope."

Blarik marveled at how the thing fit on his arm. His people never had anything like this. He rapped his knuckles on the armored plating that went to his elbow. It was just like the metal skins that he had heard about the humans wearing.

Tibbs slid the other gauntlet on Blarik's right hand. "This one is for punching. There are some metal plates on this side too, but they won't stop much more than a glancing blow. But this one is lighter and you should be able to strike fast and do some damage."

A shot from the other ship thundered through the air. "Get down!"

Blarik ducked low. Tibbs covered his head. The heavy shot ripped through rigging and splintered wood. "That one hit the forecastle. They are leading us."

Blarik tried to understand all that the gnome was saying. But, he found himself growing angry instead. Swila was on this boat. One of those fools from the other ship could hurt her. That fact alone made Blarik thirst to feel their skulls pop under his hooves like Hornel."When they come?"

Tibbs lifted up slowly. He started to finish strapping the gauntlets onto Blarik. "Pay attention If something happens, you will need to be able to put these on yourself."

Blarik watched closely. The difficult part would be the left gauntlet and forearm bracer. But, there were only three straps.

It seemed simple enough.

"Now, come on, let's get to the fantail with the captain."

The quarterdeck seemed barren. Small bits of splintered wood littered the deck from the cannon ball hit but Blarik couldn't see any direct damage. Off of the port bow he could see the other ship. They was in a tight turn, circling them. He kept his eye on a ship that was slightly larger the Undaunted as Tibbs led him up the stairs to the deck. "Mr. Tibbs, they are using a very dishonorable method to engage us."

Tibbs watched as the other ship struggled to turn to port as well. Both ships trying to maneuver against the other for a broadside gun blast. "It would seem they are using the Kha-

Harkia man-o-war tactic, same as us."

Tarrar nodded and slipped his arms into his black suit coat. The fanciful gold rim seemed to shimmer in the afternoon sun. "Aye, the scurvy dogs."

Blarik frowned "But we use it, so it okay?"

"Of course it's okay for us, we have no maritime rules of engagements. We are the Undaunted."

Blarik moved to the rail of the conning deck behind the quartermaster's shack and watched the other ship cut through the seas. It seemed so different than the Undaunted. It was adorned with bright colors and flew a bright red flag with a black eagle on it. "What flag mean?"

"Privateers, boy."

"Aye, Mr. Tibbs is right. These scum be hired to break our keels."

Tibbs grabbed Blarik by the arm. "Come boy we wait in the leech's quarters with Swila and Jenison."

Blarik nodded and followed Tibbs back down the stairs and into the sick bay. Swila rushed to him and placed her arms around him. She soaked up his warmth. He had grown so tall in the last week. She could no longer look him in the eye. She laid her head on the fine white fur of his neck, just under his chin.

"What's it look like out there, Mr. Tibbs?" Jenison placed stacks of bandages in several small barrels next to the blood stained operating table.

"They are using our Kai-Harkian man-o-war tactic." "Pirates?" Jenison arched an eyebrow.

"Worse, Privateers."

Jenison pounded his fist into his palm. "Filthy soulless bastards."

A shot echoed. Everyone ducked low. Blarik covered Swila with his body. A few moments later a soft zing could be heard in the air that grew steadily louder until it slammed into the ship, bits of wood smacked against the side of the sick bay's walls.

"Damn, twelve pounders." Tibbs growled.

"What's that?" Swila peeked out from under Blarik's arm.

Tibbs crawled out from under the Leech's table. "Guns are named based on the weight of their shot, the smaller the weight , the greater the range. Well, unless you get crazy big like a twenty pounder, but I don't know any ships that can maintain a gun that size."

"Why use twelves?" Blarik frowned.

"The larger the shot, the more damage they do. Nine pounders are designed to rip up rigging and kill sailors. That means they want to take the ship."

"What do twelve pounders do?"

Tibbs lowered his voice. "They sink you."

Jenison started to respond but was interrupted by heavy cannon blasts from the gun deck. Tibbs cheered. "Ha! We got broadside first! Let 'em have it, boys!"

The thundering cannons of the other ship answered. Heavy shots ripped through the sick bay wall, showering them with splinters.

"Stay down!" Tibbs pulled Jenison low.

The Undaunted answered back with a second cannon volley, then a third.

"We shoot faster." Blarik growled.

Tibbs nodded. "Yes, we keep our guns on a rotating rail. We can fire two volleys to their one. Plus, the track allows us to shift guns to either side."

A second round of enemy cannon blasts ripped into the Undaunted. Screams of anguish echoed from the decks below but were drowned out by two more rounds of blasts into the enemy ship.

Round after round echoed back and forth between the vessels. Screams and cries hung on the air like a slow orchestra, a choir of misery and death. After scores of minutes, the cannons round slowed.

"Get ready for the whistle, Blarik."

"Whistle?"

"Aye, when the whistle sounds, we emerge and either board or repel boarders, depending on the damage we have." "Swila's been hit!" Jenison called out.

Blarik frantically looked at Swila. A small piece of wood stuck out from her thigh.

"I'm okay."

Jenison crawled over the operating table. He pulled a bandage and a small ceramic bottle from the wooden cask. He pulled the top off with his teeth and spit the cork onto the floor. "Crawl over here. We need to soak that as soon as we can. If infection gets in there it will be the death of you."

Swila slid over to him as he soaked the bandage in rum.

"Hold this. When I pull the wood out, place this over it." Tibbs crawled toward the door. "Come on Blarik." He glanced back at Swila then to Tibbs.

"Look, blue boy. You can sit in here and do nothing, or you can get yer arse out on deck and make those bastards pay."

Blarik growled and stood.

"Get down fool." Tibbs warned.

Blarik went to the door. He tried to open it with his awkward gauntleted hand. After a few attempts he kicked the door open. Bits of wood cracked and popped from the frame. The door splintered and fell to the deck. Blarik turned to Tibbs, his blue eyes filled with fury. "You coming, Mr. Tibbs?"

WHITE WRATH

Blarik stepped out onto the quarterdeck. He almost didn't recognize it. The bulwark was splintered and ripped up. The forward mast was cracked and leaning to port. Loose rigging hung torn and frayed.

"Stay low Blarik." Tibbs crept from the door to the edge of the aft bulwark.

Blarik moved his gaze to the other ship. Their crew was moving planks and ladders on their deck. Their port side was peppered with splintered wood and holes. Their gun decks had gaping holes. He could see mangled twisted bodies lying amidst torn and scattered cannons.

A shrill whistle sounded from the Undaunted's fantail. "There's our cue, boy."

The men from the line locker erupted from below. They yelled and screamed, waving their swords and axes. The men from the other ship did the same. Both twirled grappling hooks and tossed them toward the other ship.

"What they doing, Mr. Tibbs?"

"Grapples, boy. We have moved close enough that their twelve pounders couldn't hit us below the water line. So our gun decks took turns blasting one another until the gun crews were disabled enough that the only option is to fight. Now, we grapple. The winner gets both ships."

Blarik watched in amazement as both ships worked together to secure the other's grapple. They seemed so eager to help each other get to the fight. The men heaved and strained pulling both ships close enough together to place narrow planks between them. Blarik watched both ships slide huge nets over the side.

"Nets?" Blarik peeked around the bulwark.

"Aye, in case we fall over, we climb up the netting."

"Won't they climb up?"

"Aye, but our belief is that our men are better fighters, so it's to our advantage to recover them."

Shouts and threats echoed out from the two ships. The men paused on both sides at the edge of the planks. Captain Tarrar emerged from the conning shack and stood at the edge.

"There's their captain." Tibbs pointed at a chubby man with long blonde hair.

"What he doing?"

"The other ship is the attacker, so he is offering a silent chance to surrender. We will stand firm. The other captain will wait until for some time to pass."

Cheers erupted from the ship.

"What that"

Tibbs smiled. "Well, that could happen too."

"What?"

Tibbs pointed up to Captain Tarrar. "He could insult them by turning his back. He is pretty much saying that he needs not tend to the battle, that it is already won."

Blarik sighed. "That relieving. I was nervous."

"No, boy. It doesn't mean we win. It means Tarrar is boasting that we will win." Tibbs chuckled.

Blarik watched the men charge across the planks. They met in the middle in a clash of swordplay. "If we might lose, why boast? Seems silly."

Tibbs grabbed his two axes and stepped from the behind the bulwark. "We won't lose boy."

Blarik stood from the side of the ship and stepped out next to Tibbs. "How do you know?"

Tibbs moved up the stairs to the deck. "Because if we lose, we die. Now, let's get ready to fling."

Blarik watched Tibbs take hold of a line that hung down from the rear mast. Two men grabbed the line that fed up to the mast, through a pulley and was connected to Tibbs. The little gnome ran and leapt over the edge of the ship. The two men jerked hard on the line and sent Tibbs sailing into the air. The little gnome landed roughly on the other side. He jumped to his feet and immediately engaged the men on the other side with his twin axes.

"You ready, Blarik?" One of the two men holding the line asked.

Blarik grabbed the line. It was thick and awkward. He couldn't get a very good grip with his right hand and his left one was encased in the heavy metal plating. He wrapped the line around his wrist several times and pulled on it. The line was taught and seemed secured to him. He took a deep breath.

"Ready."

"On your leap, Blarik."

Blarik flexed his powerful leg muscles and ran across the conning deck. His hard heavy hooves thundered across the deck. He stepped up on the rail in mid stride and leapt into the air. The two men heaved on the line. Blarik launched up in the air slightly but his weight was too great. The 2 men were pulled forward and lost their footing. The heavy line pulled the first man's arm into the pulley. The force wedged it into the metal casing. The man screamed as his skin was shucked off of his forearm. It bunched up to his shoulder.

Blarik felt himself rocket up into the air, but then suddenly dropped. He watched as he descended far below the other ship's fantail. It looked like he would smack into the side of the ship. At the last moment, the line went taught and jerked him to the side. Pain erupted in his shoulder and elbow. Blarik's momentum launched him into a cannon hole on the gun deck level.

His hard hooves slid out from under him and he skidded into a damaged gun cart. He wasn't sure what happened. He thought he was supposed to land on the other ship's fantail with Tibbs.

Blarik got to his feet. His shoulder burned and his hand was numb. He tried to unwind the rope, but the line was ripped tight. He shook his left arm to get the gauntlet off so he could untie it, but the straps held the armor in place. Blarik felt ridiculous and angry.

Two men emerged from a side locker. They were pushing a cart with two barrels on it. It looked like the powder barrels that they kept on the Undaunted. The men paused when they saw Blarik.

The minotaur sneered. "You are the ones that were shooting. You hurt Swila."

The men looked at one another uneasily. "Look! He's stuck to his line."

The other laughed. "Get that nine pounder. Let's give him an ass load of steel."

Blarik watched the men slide a smaller cannon from the aft area of the deck toward him. One sponged out the barrel while the other prepared the powder. It dawned on him they were going to shoot him. He struggled and pulled on the line as hard as he could, but he couldn't seem to free himself.

One man packed the nine-pound charge into the barrel while the other laughed. Blarik frantically looked for someplace to hide. He tugged on the rope, but it would not budge. Blarik watched in horror as the men lit the fuse. It burned agonizing slow as the men laughed and mocked him. It reminded him of his mother. She would laugh and mock him.

The fuse disappeared under the cannon's lip. Blarik closed his eyes and lifted the small metal shield plate on his left arm and covered his face. The cannon exploded. Blarik felt small pieces of shot rip through his body. It felt like a hundred giant bee stings. Blarik lowered his shield arm. Heavy pieces of steel embedded themselves into the plating. He was bleeding from his chest, his thighs, and his shoulder.

They laughed. "Let's get our twenty pounder."

Rage filled Blarik. Rage like when he killed Hornel, but amplified tenfold. He flexed his muscles and pulled on the rope with all his might. The line creaked and gave way. Blarik lurched forward. The men jumped back. Blarik regained his balance and charged.

One of the cannoneers fled but the other was frozen in fear. He placed his hands up defensively as Blarik charged in. The bull lowered his head and rammed into the sailor. Blarik's heavy horned skull crashed into the man, crushing his head and shoulders. The starboard bulkhead of the ship cracked under the force of the blow. Warm bits of blood and skull showered Blarik in a bath of gore. The young bull turned his rage to the other man.

The terrified sailor drew his scimitar and backed into a corner. Blarik didn't say anything. He stalked forward. The sailor stabbed out. Blarik turned the blade with his plated arm and punched with the other. The heavy gauntlet struck the sailor in the face. The force of the blow crushed his lower jaw and pinned his head to the wall. Blood squirted from the wound and sprayed Blarik's face. He flexed his arm and stared at the man. He was sick with pain and seemed semiconscious. Blarik thought of Swila. He growled and gored the man with his horn. The hard bony spike ripped a hole in the sailor's face. Blarik let him fall to the deck. The dying man made quick gasps for a few seconds before Blarik stomped on his head. The young bull relished the sweet smell. He'd thought it stunk at first, but it seemed to arouse him now. Thick with the fervor of battle, Blarik stalked up the stairs to the conning deck.

***

Tibbs ducked an awkward slash and brought his axe down on the man's foot. The razor sharp blade neatly sliced off the front half of the man's foot. Tibbs ignored the disabled sailor and deflected a hammer strike from another. His second axe came in angled low, and took off the sailor's leg in mid shin. The wounded man screamed in pain and grabbed his bloody nub.

Tibbs advanced toward the captain. "Ask me for parley, old man."

The Captain chuckled. "The infamous Mr. Tibbs."

Tibbs mock bowed. "I am at disadvantage, sir. I know not your name."

The Captain gestured behind Tibbs and calmly uncorked a bottle of rum. "A double disadvantage, Mr. Tibbs. Your men are being bested and your ship is cracked below the waterline."

Tibbs moved back over to the rail and looked. The Undaunted was being overrun. Their sailors had been pushed from the quarterdeck and now formed defensive lines at the aft and the forecastle.

"Shit."

"Indeed," the Captain said. He poured a second goblet of rum.

***

Blarik ducked low under a beam. A cannon ball had torn a hole in the stairwell wall revealing stairs that spiraled around a pole and went up. Blarik squeezed through the narrow space and made his way upwards. The stairs ended in a small room.

Blarik sniffed at the door. He couldn't seem to find a handle like the doors on the Undaunted. He pushed on the door lightly until he discovered that it slid. He wedged his thick fingers in the edge of the door and slid it open revealing what looked quite similar to the conning shack on his ship. Blarik spied Tibbs against the rail and the enemy captain.

Blarik emerged from the shack. His hard hooves clicked across the deck.

"Blarik!" Tibbs called out.

The captain turned and regarded the white minotaur. "So when did you begin training livestock?"

Blarik frowned. "Mr. Tibbs, is this the bad captain?"

Tibbs nodded. "Aye."

Without a word, Blarik stabbed the two spikes from his left hand into the face of the Captain. The shocked sailor quivered and shuddered before sliding from the blades to a lifeless form on the deck. Blarik stepped over the Captain and stomped his head. Bits of skull and matter squirted across the deck, but with much better distance than the others. Blarik was perfecting the head stomp quite nicely.

"What the fuck, Blarik!?"

Blarik grabbed one of the goblets and gulped down the rum. "What you mean, Mr. Tibbs?"

"You just face fucked the captain!"

Blarik glanced down at the captain's lifeless form. "Aye, I guess I did."

Tibbs was beside himself. "You can't kill the captains!"

Blarik shrugged. "He tried to hurt Swila and his men tried to hurt you."

"No, I mean, it's against the rules to kill the captain."

Blarik moved next to Tibbs and handed him the other goblet of rum. "We need to get back over to our ship. We are losing."

"We will all be killed for sure once the men realize you killed their captain." Tibbs stood in shock.

Blarik walked back over to the dead captain. "Why?"

"It will send them into a fervor and they are about to take the Undaunted."

Blarik pondered the way his father used to hunt skrull. He lifted the body of the dead Captain and carried it to the rail. He hoisted it high in the air, "Look!" He shouted. "I killed your weak captain."

The fighting on the other ship slowed as the hordes of enemy sailors tried to gage if the mangled corpse was really their captain.

Tibbs placed his hand on his forehead. "You have to be the dumbest creature alive."

Blarik glanced down. "No, Tibbs. Like skrull hunting. Make big male mad and he chase. Then you raid den."

The realization of what the boy was proposing washed over him. "Brilliant, boy blue. Well done!"

Blarik nodded and turned back to the Undaunted. "Next I am going to bed captain like sweet lover." Blarik recalled hearing a bull say that to his father before. It enraged his father so much he'd killed the other bull. Much to Blarik's pleasure, the men began to abandon the Undaunted. It seemed like they could not get back across the planks fast enough.

Tibbs watched the captain lower a thin rope ladder of the side of the conning deck. "Quick boy, we have to disable this ship somehow."

Blarik tossed the body of the Captain overboard sending the charging men into a greater rage.

Tibbs laughed to himself. Yes, this boy was going to make a fine pirate. "Grab that wheel. It's the helm. If we can smash it or damage it, it will take them days to repair it and give us time to escape."

Blarik pulled on the helm and punched the wooden sprocket holding it while Tibbs chopped at it with abandon. When one of the wheels came loose, Blarik tossed it over the side and they started work on the other one. In moments, it was loose as well. Tibbs chopped at some rigging as Blarik tossed the second helm of the side. Just as the men reached the conning deck, they caught a glimpse of Tibbs and Blarik hurling themselves over the edge and into the sea.

Blarik was surprised the water was as cold as it was. He swam to the rope ladder. "Grab my neck, Mr. Tibbs!" Tibb's wrapped his arms around Blarik's neck and climbed onto his back.

Blarik scampered up the awkward ladder and was helped onto the conning deck. The other sailors were already trying to reestablish planks, but the Undaunted sailors kept dislodging them.

Captain Tarrar gave Blarik a nasty glare. "Jenison, summon us a wind and get us out of here."

The mage thumbed his holy symbol and said a prayer. The air around his outstretched distorted and a great wind appeared from nowhere and filled the sails of the ship. In moments, the Undaunted sailed away from the crippled vessel that had nearly captured them.

UNDERWAY

Blarik stood at attention on the conning deck just as Tibbs had shown him. The little gnome argued with the Captain so furiously, he wasn't sure half of what they were saying.

"I don't care, Captain. If the boy hadn't killed their skipper, you would likely be getting a good view of the underside of their ship!"

The captain slammed his fist down on the quartermaster's table. "Do you think I don't know that? But to what end? He has surely pissed in the face of the gods. Surshy was at odds with us before going into this little battle. Now, we have violated the combat terms of the maritime code. Aside from word getting out that the Undaunted has no code, the gods will surely sink us before other pirates start preying on us."

Blarik's knees ached. Standing in the odd position made him a bit dizzy.

Tibbs shook his head. "We don't even know what the name of that vessel was. They fly under a privateer banner, but claimed no nation. That alone is breaking our code. They broke it first."

The captain rubbed his chin. "I see that point, but even then, that is in stark contrast to murdering their captain."

"Aye Captain, but may I tell you something?"

"We are speaking familiar, Mr. Tibbs. else you would be tied to the masthead."

Tibbs smiled. "Well, Captain. When I saw those men closing on your position, I was about to kill their captain myself. I'd rather die a renegade pirate than a slave on my own ship."

Tarrar nodded quietly. "Aye."

"So, Captain, the boy didn't do anything that we wouldn't have. He simply did it in a gruesome and effective manner that will surely incite fear and reverence into the prowess of your crew."

Captain Tarrar walked back to the helm in silence. The warm southern wind zipped by them. The ship was repaired as best they could without new lumber. The holes were shored up and Jenison assured them he had enough scrolls created to keep them full speed ahead for a week. Though, they would need to stop for supplies around that time. "Mr. Tibbs."

"Yes, Captain?"

"Get the hell off of my deck and take that thing with you."

Tibbs smiled wide. "Aye sir." He motioned to Blarik.

"Come on, we got work to do."

***

The next week went remarkably fast for Blarik. He and Tibbs fished off of the fantail. Blarik was hungrier than ever. He ate three times that of one the other sailors. He was growing closer to Swila, but she seemed to be becoming increasingly distant. He knew she missed her home and her family.

Blarik began to enjoy his routine. He would wake in the morning and learn combat with Tibbs. In the afternoon he learned more human words with Swila. She was an excellent teacher. After the third meal, Blarik would sit on the fantail with Swila and watch the sun set. She would speak to him in his own language.

He really enjoyed that time. She would lean up against him and lay her head on his shoulder. She held his hand last night. It was an odd experience. Blarik didn't see a point to it, but having his finger interlocked with hers made it seem like they were sharing a bond that he couldn't explain.

"Mr. Tibbs, how old do you have to be to take a wife?"

Tibbs baited his hook with a piece of meat. "Well, you need to be a man first."

100

Blarik frowned. "How do you become a man?"

"It's an age thing. When you reach a certain age, you just are a man."

"Am I there yet?"

Tibbs tossed his line out to sea. The weighted hook flipped end over end before splashing into the deep blue water.

"Blarik, what are you asking?"

Blarik bit his lip. "Well, Swila has been my friend…"

"Whoa, hold on, boy. Swila is a human."

Blarik nodded. "Yes."

"You are not a human."

"Yes."

Tibbs laughed. "Blarik you cannot marry someone outside of your race."

Blarik felt his heart sink. "Why not?"

"Well, for starters, you have to be able to make love to them."

"How do you know when you have made love? I think Swila and I have made it."

Tibbs was surprised at first then relaxed. He took a draw from the ceramic jug of rum. "No, boy. You and she have not made love."

"Well, we hold hands at night."

Tibbs clapped Blarik on the shoulder. "Boy, that's not making love."

"So how do you make love?"

"Um…"

Blarik hoisted the jug and took a sip. The bottle was not shaped for his mouth, so had to pour a long draw in.

"Blarik, …well. Damn. Why are you asking me this?"

Blarik shrugged. "You're my friend."

"Okay, remember when we first met and I wanted you to cover up that hammer of yours?"

"Hammer?"

Tibbs sighed. "Hammer, man. Hammer. That thing you pee with. Ya know?" Tibbs was flustered.

Blarik nodded. "Yes, Swila made me the lion cloth."

"Yea, and it's 'loin' cloth."

Blarik tugged on his line a bit. "Yes, that. She said without she couldn't hug me."

"Yea, well. ...In order to make love, you have to put your hammer in her ...hammer holder."

Blarik frowned. "It doesn't come off, Mr. Tibbs."

"By the gods, man, didn't your cow parents teach you anything?"

Blarik slumped his shoulders. "No, I was a disgrace to them. I was not even allowed to cook."

"A disgrace, why?"

Blarik explained the story of his youth. He recounted the tales of the beatings and meeting Swila. He told him about all the years of sneaking away and spending the day with her. He told of the fateful day he ran away and when his father attacked. Tibbs felt a profound sadness at the abuse this poor boy had suffered.

"Well, boy. I don't know when you are old enough, but based on how much you have been growing lately, I'd think your stones are about to drop."

"My stones?"

"It's just a saying, boy. Look, here is the deal. Cut and dry. Making love is a way two people who love one another express that love."

Blarik nodded. "I see, like a normal hug versus a long one with hard squeezes."

"Yea, kind of."

"So how do you make this love? Is it hard?"

"No boy, you'll find that once you get going, it will come naturally."

"So how do you get going?"

"Well, like I said, females have a hammer holder. It's between their legs. When the time is right and she wants to make love to you, she will have you put your hammer in there."

Blarik nodded. "I see. Seems a bit silly, but okay."

"Oh, it's quite silly, boy. But it's also so coveted that nations have killed thousands of people because they wanted the hammer holder that one particular women had."

"I don't think I want to make love, Mr. Tibbs. Sounds embarrassing."

102

Tibbs chuckled. "It can be. Oh, there is something else that comes with it."

Blarik felt a jerk on his line. "I think I caught a fish."

Tibbs watched the innocent monster next to him. It was odd to see a boy so young one moment and the cold-blooded monster he was on the enemy ship the next. "Bring it on in, Blarik."

"I hope it's a big one. I'm still hungry after third meal. So, tell me what also comes with making love."

"Well, boy. If you're not careful, making love can make a baby."

Blarik stop pulling in the fish. He turned and faced the gnome. He cocked his head to the side. "A baby? How does it do that?"

Tibbs groaned. "Me and my big mouth. Look, I'm not getting into it now, Blarik. We can cover that topic when I have more rum."

Blarik pulled the fish on board. "Okay, Mr. Tibbs. You clean the fish and I'll find more rum. Making babies sounds fascinating."

Tibbs dropped his face in his palm and watched the Minotaur scurry off. This was going to be a long evening.

***

Blarik found it odd; Swila had not come to the fantail with him. She was normally there before sunset. The young bull made his way below decks and to the rum locker. He fumbled with the keys that Tibbs had given him and unlocked the locker.

His keen ears heard an odd muffled sound. He paused for a moment before removing the lock. He opened the door and reached for a jug, when he heard it again. It was coming from the forward line locker. Blarik took out a ceramic jug of rum and placed it on the deck. He relocked the locker and picked up the jug. As he started up the stairs, it sounded like someone crying. Blarik paused and listened again. He cocked his head to the side and his large white ears turned toward the sound. Was someone hurt? He moved around the stairs and started down toward the line locker.

He heard the muffled cries and a heavy voice. "Keep your mouth shut, bitch."

Blarik's moved faster. The voice sounded angry. He reached for the line locker door, but it wouldn't open. "What's going on?"

"Blarik, help me!"

Blarik dropped the ceramic jug. Warm rum erupted from the broken jar. That was Swila's voice.

Rage filled him. He punched the door lock. The brass hand bent down, the wood of the line locker door shattered. The young bull shouldered through the door. The locker was more of a large room. Piles of thick heavy mooring lines were coiled up on the deck. Swila lay on her back. She seemed weak and she was pulling up her pants. "Blarik," she cried. "He was trying to hurt me."

Blarik scanned the room; he caught the glimpse of a boot sliding out of a small porthole near the top of the room. Rage filled him. He was drunk with fury. The young bull charged up the heavy coiled lines. The foot slid through the hole, but Blarik kept his charge. He lowered his head and rammed into the bulkhead. The force of his blow carried him through the opening and onto the other side.

Blarik opened his eyes and was surprised to see that he was outside of the ship. Bits of wood and debris were all around him. The flailing body of the man was too, and they both were falling into the ocean. Blarik eagerly awaited the plunge into the water so he could catch the man.

The cold ocean washed over him. Blarik opened his eyes and ignored the sting in his eyes. He could see the man swimming to the surface. Blarik kicked his legs and paddled.

He broke surface and swam after the man.

"It wasn't what you think, Blarik."

Blarik ignored the man's pleading as he tried to escape. Swila said he was trying to hurt her and he would die for it.

The man grabbed a plank of wood and started kicking away from the ship. Bells sounded on the Undaunted and men's voices echoed behind him, but he would not deviate from his task.

The frantic sailor screamed and begged for mercy as he tried to escape. Blarik reached out and grabbed the sailor by his foot and pulled him from his plank. The man struck Blarik in the face. Blarik ignored the weak blow and grabbed the sailor by the back of the head.

He pulled him close and bit at his face. His heavy teeth scraped the sailor's soft skin and clamped down on his nose. Blarik bit down. He could feel the nose crunch in his mouth and the eruption of salty blood. The man screamed and gurgled as they sunk into the depths of the water.

The sailor tried to escape and Blarik bit his neck. His dull flat teeth grabbed the sailor's soft flesh. Blood erupted from the bite and shot jets of red into the sea depths. When the man stopped struggling, Blarik released him. He gave the body one last glimpse as it sunk into the ocean depths.

Blarik spit out the dead sailor's nose and broke the surface. He started swimming back to the boat. It had turned in the water and was coming back for him. The Undaunted looked so beautiful in the sea. Much like the first day he seen it. He waited patiently for the ship to come alongside. Tibbs learned over the rail and tossed him a rope ladder. Blarik climbed up the device to the deck. His white fur dripped on the deck.

Tibbs handed him a towel. "What the hell was that?"

Captain Tarrar stormed toward him. "Why is their hole in my line locker bulkhead? Why is the girl crying, and why in the hell are you in the drink?"

"He was trying to hurt Swila. I chased him and he tried escape. I ran to grab him as he was climbing out of a porthole. The wall broke and we fell into the sea."

"So, where is he now?"

Tibbs interjected. "Prolly the same place as everyone else that clashes with the boy's wrath, dead"

"God dammit, Mr. Tibbs. We are out of lumber and if the seas get heavy, sea spray is going to soak our mooring lines."

Tibbs nodded. "Blarik, dismantle yer bunk. You will use that wood to repair the hole you made."

"Aye Mr. Tibbs."

"That's it?" One sailor groaned. "He kills Jackabe and he has to dismantle his bunk? He should be tied to the masthead for a fortnight at the very least!"

"Jackabe tried to rape Swila." Tibbs growled.

The crewmembers seemed unconcerned. "So? That little whore shouldn't be onboard anyway."

Tibbs tensed. He expected Blarik to attack the man, but the young bull continued on his trek below. "This is not a debate. Get back to your duties."

The sailors groaned, but dispersed.

"This may get worse before it gets better, Mr. Tibbs." Captain Tarrar leaned against the quarterdeck rail. He gazed out to sea distantly.

Tibbs picked up a towel and tossed it over his shoulder. "Aye. But he will learn."

"No, Blarik isn't the problem."

"Captain?"

Captain Tarrar unscrewed the lid from his flask. The steel case shimmered in the evening light. "How is the boy coming with his studies?"

Tibbs was confused. "Quite well. He is much smarter than we gave him credit for. But, what does that have to do with him being a problem. I mean, who is the problem, sir?"

"The girl. That's why we are sailing back to New Gradenbach."

"Sir, you know that's a hub for Kingston Naval vessels."

"Of course I do, Mr. Tibbs. But, there is no way to keep Blarik onboard unless we take her home. He would not let go of her any other way."

"I'm not so sure that even taking her home will work. He was asking about making love."

The captain laughed. "That's actually a good sign. Shows his stones are dropping. Aside from his lust, his rage will be growing too."

"I don't think that's his motive, sir. I think he genuinely loves her."

106

"Gag me with the shark god's cock."

Tibbs nodded. "But, he seems to have taking a liking to the ship. As long as we can mitigate the crews clashes with him, I think he will choose to stay us. I don't think he wants to go home."

"Oh? Why is that, Mr. Tibbs?"

Tibbs watched Blarik come up from below. He had his bunk under his arm. It appeared as if he simply ripped the heavy wooden rack from the bulkhead. "He told me about his family. It was one of abuse and disgrace. If he goes back, they will kill him."

"Well, the people of New Gradenbach won't take him. They have violent battles with the minotaur tribes fairly often. In fact, we will likely have to fend them off if they learn he is on board."

Tibbs nodded. "That could be a good excuse to secure the docks and take what supplies we can get our hands on. They see Blarik and attack. We secure the docks, and use Jenison's wind to get out fast."

"Aye, tis a grand plan Mr. Tibbs."

"So, when do we arrive, sir?"

The captain took another long draw from his flask. "Based on the quartermaster's charts, I'd say sometime tomorrow morning. That is as long as the wind holds."

HOMECOMING

Blarik walked below "Swila?"

"I'm here, Blarik."

He walked to his bunk. Swila sat there, she looked upset and disheveled but not injured. Blarik sat next to her. He placed his arm around her. She seemed so small and frail to him. "Are you okay, Kim?"

She glanced up and smiled through her tears. She spoke to him in his own language. "I'm okay, Blaro. But, I want to go home. I miss my family so bad. I try not to blame you, but if I had not helped you, none of this would have ever happened."

The truth hit Blarik harder than any beating he ever faced. "I'm sorry."

The two words resonated with Swila. Blarik had never had anything. His life had been one suffering event after another. "Blaro, this isn't your fault. Well, not like faults in the way of intentional."

"Then how?"

Swila cried. Her sobs ripped a hole in his heart and every tear that drained from her face weakened him like blood lost from his veins. "Swila. After I repair the hole I made, I will go to the captain. He will turn the ship around and take you home."

"He would never do that. They are pirates."

Blarik had no idea what a pirate was. "Swila, they are my friends. I will tell them that's important to me."

Swila glared at him. "Blarik, you have to stop being fool. They want you as a weapon. Nothing more. You are a tool to them. You will be discarded as soon as you are no longer useful."

Blarik growled. He grabbed Swila by her shoulders and lifted her from his rack. He placed his heavy hoofed foot against the bulk and grabbed his rack. With a feral growl, he pulled. The wood creaked and splintered as it was torn from the bulkhead.

Blarik sneered at her. "I'll do as I said. I'll tell them to take you home. If they refuse, we will leave the ship and I will find a way to take you home myself."

Swila was amazed at the raw power wrapped in body with such a soft heart. "Okay, Blaro."

Blarik was a bit confused at her quick agreement. "Yea, so that's what I'm going to do."

Swila wiped a tear from her face. "Okay, Blaro."

Blarik stared at her a few more moments waiting for her to fire some sort of retort. When she didn't, he sneered and stormed up the stairs.

Blarik emerged on the quarterdeck carrying his rack. The ropes that held the rack upright dangled behind, still attached to portions of the bulkhead. Blarik's heavy hooves stomped on the deck. He marched to the forecastle and tossed down the bunk. He leaned over the bulwark.

"So, what are you doing, Blarik?"

Blarik turned to see Tibbs standing looking at him with a cock-eyed smile on his face. "I'm fixing this damned hole."

Tibbs stifled a chuckle. "Something got you flustered, Blarik? Is Swila okay?"

"She's FINE."

"So...wouldn't it be easier to fix the hole from the inside?"

Blarik turned and placed his hands on his hips. He fired off in his own language. "I mean, she says it's my fault she is stuck on this ship. I didn't make her get in the boat. I didn't make things go the way they did. What about me?"

Tibbs blinked. Blarik's language sounded so vicious. "Um, I don't speak that drivel."

Blarik paused briefly,. "Sorry Mr. Tibbs. Swila is fine. She is unhappy here and blames me. After I fix this hole, I am going to go to the captain and tell him he needs to take her home."

"Well, I can do that for you, boy. I mean, I know the captain well. I can word it in such a way that he would listen. Plus, we aren't far from the island anyway. We had to head this way after the fight with the privateer ship."

Blarik felt a huge weight lift from his shoulders. "If I could smile, Mr. Tibbs, I would." He rubbed the little gnome on the head and picked up the bunk. "Let's go fix that hole."

Tibbs fixed adjusted his hat. "You fix the hole, blue boy. I'll go speak to the captain."

***

Captain Tarrar propped his salty boots up on his desk and leaned back in his rocking chair he'd bought in Harbor Mountain a few years ago. "So you say the boy wants us to get rid of her?" The captain was astounded.

"He wants us to take her home." Tibbs corrected. "He wants what's best for her."

"Does he plan to leave the ship too?"

Tibbs chuckled. "Only if we don't get rid of the girl."

"The god's shine favor on us, Mr. Tibbs!"

"Aye, they do."

Captain Tarrar paused. "Does he want to return home himself?"

"No, Captain. He was mistreated in his tribe like a man might mistreat a lame slave. He likes it here with us."

"I don't like that he thinks he can hold us hostage. He should have been killed on sight, or made a slave at the very least."

Tibbs leaned forward on the Captain's table. "Don't let pride get in the way here, Captain. He knows none of these things, so how could he be appreciative of them?"

"Aye. A fair point, Mr. Tibbs. Go tell the boy that we will take his beloved home as long as he will pledge loyalty to me and my ship until death."

Tibbs nodded and placed his cap back on his head.

"Consider it a done deal, Captain."

***

Blarik stared at the hammer. It was an odd contraption. It had no resemblance to any part of his body. He picked up the tool and held it in his hand. He steadied the nail and lightly tapped it. In no time the nail was buried into the plank. He repeated this process several times until the top portion of the hole was covered. Blarik kneeled on the heavy coiled mooring line and peered out of the hole. The sky was lit with oranges and blues, but he couldn't see the sunset.

He missed Swila. Even if she was going home and he would likely never see her again, those weeks sitting on the fantail with her were the happiest days of his life. He sighed and grabbed another plank.

"Hey, boy."

Blarik ignored the little gnome.

"Got some good news for you."

"Mr. Tibbs, there is no good news for me. Either my best friend is staying on ship and hating me forever, or she is getting her desire and leaving me forever. Neither can be good news."

Tibbs bit his lip and climbed up the coiled mooring lines.

He handed Blarik one of the wooden planks. "You love her?" Blarik hammered the nail in rather violently.

"I think you do. You may not know what love is, but the fact you are willing to put your wants and needs aside for what's best for her. That's love, boy."

Blarik pulled a nail from his mouth and hammered in another plank. "The sunsets were ours, Mr. Tibbs. And every nail I drive into this ship, to repair it, is a one step closer to burying those sunset's forever."

Tibbs handed Blarik another plank. "Aye. But would you rather have her with you, and miserable? A prisoner to your feelings?"

Blarik placed the nail against the wood and with one strike, drove the nail home. "No."

Tibbs clapped him on the back. "Welcome to being a man."

112

Blarik narrowed his eyes and turned to face Tibbs. "I am no man, Mr. Tibbs. I am a minotaur.

The gnome almost felt a murderous hate burning from those blue orbs. "Yes. Yes you are."

Blarik turned back to his task. "So is the captain going to take her home?"

"Aye."

Blarik pounded in the last nail of the plank. He ran his fingers over the hole. It seemed secure. "When will we arrive?"

"Tomorrow morning, most likely."

Blarik felt his heart sink. "So soon?"

"Yes, we were forced to sail in this direction already. New Gradenbach is fairly close to here."

Blarik handed the hammer to Tibbs. "I'll go tell Swila. Maybe she will spend one last night with me on the fantail."

Tibbs nodded. His heart hurt for the boy. "Don't waste it with hurt and anger. Be gracious and suck it all in like a good steak. Eventually it'll be gone, but make sure you enjoy every bite."

Blarik paused at the door to the line locker. "What's a steak, Mr. Tibbs?"

Tibbs felt his face go red. "It's uh… a food. Don't worry about it. Forget I said it. But, do you get what I mean?"

"Aye." Blarik rubbed his chest. The anxiety was rushing through his veins. He walked from the line locker up to the berthing area. The ship's crew was crowded around a small circle. They were tossing the dice again. They paid Blarik no mind and the young bull made his way up the stairs to the quarterdeck and then the Swila's berth in sick bay. He knocked on the door. The sound of his knuckles hitting the wood echoed like the sound of the executioner's gong.

"Be right there."

Blarik forced himself to wear his most pleasant face. Swila opened the door and stood face to face with the middle of Blarik's muscular chest. She looked up. The young bull seemed visibly upset. Most might not be able to tell, but she had known Blarik a long time. "What's wrong, Blarik?"

"The Captain says we are on our way to take you home."

Swila felt her eyes well up with tears. She wrapped her arms around Blarik's waist and hugged him tight. "But why do you seem so sad? Because I'm leaving?"

Blarik nodded. "Yes, you're my best friend."

Swila took Blarik by the hand and led him from her chamber. "Let's go to the fantail. The sun will set soon, but we can watch the sky change."

Blarik followed her. Just the sound of her voice was a gasp of breath at the bottom of the sea.

She led him to the rear of the conning deck. They leaned on the rail and watched the western sky. The wind lightly blew Swila's hair about her face. "I have never seen an angel before, Swila. But, I'd bet they look like you do right now."

Swila looked at Blarik and smiled. She stared into his bright blue eyes. She always loved them. Despite his monstrous features he always had the eyes of a gentle man. It was like she could see his soul, his tender, gentle soul. "When do you think we will be home?"

Blarik looked away and back out to the west. The last bit of the sun dipped below the ocean's horizon. "Tomorrow morning sometime," his words ended as the sun blinked under the sea.

Swila fought her excitement. She was so eager to see her family, but she knew what this meant to Blarik.

"Ya know, Kim." Blarik paused. "Mr. Tibbs told me to relish this evening. He told me to take it all in and that I would have these memories for the rest of my life. But, I don't think I want these memories. This hurts. It hurts like when momma would beat me. It hurts on the inside."

Swila moved closer and took Blarik's hand. She laid her head on his shoulder. "Blarik, I'm sorry. I really am. But, I have to go home. Isn't there some way you could make your own tribe on Kerisis? Maybe make one that works with my people instead of fights with us?"

Blarik shook his head. "No, my tribe would hunt me. I am a disgrace to them."

Swila felt her nose sting and tears started to well up in her eyes. "Blarik, this is a pirate ship. Do you know what means?" Blarik shook his head.

"It means they attack and steal from other ships. They enslave and kill people. They are not good men."

Blarik frowned. "Mr. Tibbs is a good person. Sure there are some that are not, like Hornel and Jackabe-but I will find those men and root 'em out. There are bad people in every tribe. Even your tribe."

Swila burst into tears. She buried her face into Blarik's chest. The young bull stood in shock a moment before placing his arms around her. Her touch felt good.

"Oh, Blarik. You always try to see the best in people, even when they are at their worst. Just be careful."

Blarik broke the embrace. He grabbed her by the shoulders and looked into her eyes. "Kim…," he said in her language. "I love you. I always will. But Mr. Tibbs was wrong. This is not a moment in my life I want to relish. Spending the last few hours with you is torture. I don't want to do it anymore."

He leaned in and placed his mouth on hers in his best attempt to mimic a kiss. "I'm going to my bunk. Well, what's left of it. I'm saying goodbye now. I'll not see you off in the morning and I don't want to see your people or your tribe. I don't want to try and fit in with a group that would kill me for my appearance or not accept me for the quality of my character."

Swila watched him turn and go. She was in shock. Her best friend had said the most profound words she had ever heard. She knew this was one of the moments her father talked about. One of those few moments in life that changes you. Blarik was surely one of kind. How would the world shape him?

A PIRATE'S LIFE FOR ME

The sound of the shrill boatman's whistle sounded across the decks. "Revelry."

Blarik rubbed his tired eyes. For his first few waking moments he had forgotten that this was the day Swila would leave him forever. He sat up and stretched.

The hard deck was a poor replacement for his bunk and the blanket they gave him was much too small and seemed to be grower smaller by the day. But, there was something comforting to sleeping on the hard wood floor. It reminded him of sleeping on the ground outside of his family's tent when he was a youth. He was lonely and a bit cold, but he enjoyed the sights and sounds of the world around him. And while there were no barking tree frogs or chirping crickets, the ship had its own soothing sounds, like the creak of the wood and the rhythmic sound of the waves crashing against the bow.

But, this morning there were no sounds. The ship didn't pitch and the bunks didn't creak.

ShaneMoore

Blarik got up. Most of the ship's crew was gone from their racks. Blarik started toward the door. Mr. Tibbs sat on the bottom stair of the ladder well.

"Morning, Blarik."

Blarik rubbed his head. "Where is everyone?"

"We are in port. In New Gradenbach." Tibbs sipped a cup of black liquid.

"Where is…?"

"She's gone."

Blarik sighed. He looked past Mr. Tibbs and up the stairs. The bright sun beckoned to him.

"You can't go on deck, Blarik. She isn't there and we don't want to risk what will happen if they see you."

Blarik considered going on deck anyway. His heart longed for one final glimpse of her. Maybe she was walking down the pier. Maybe he could call out to her and maybe she would turn and smile one last time.

Blarik plopped down next to Tibbs. "This sucks."

Tibbs clapped the young bull on the back. "Aye. And I'm sorry for you. Did you get to say your goodbyes last night?"

Blarik nodded distantly. "Aye. I said what needed to be said."

Tibbs unscrewed the top of a large round metal flask. He pulled a wooden mug from his pack and poured some of the black liquid into the cup. "Here," he handed the mug to Blarik.

Blarik sniffed the liquid. "What is it? It looks like wood tar but less thick like water."

"It's called coffee. Thought you might like it. It's much better hot, but warm will have to do."

Blarik tilted his head back and poured a bit of it in his mouth. "I've never tasted anything like it. It's bitter."

"Aye, but it gives you pep."

142
WhiteWraith

"Pep?"

"Yea, if you're tired or run down, a few cups of this will pep you right up."

Blarik tilted his head back and gulped the rest down. "I'm feeling particularly run down this morning, Mr. Tibbs."

"Aye, but not even a whole pot of this stuff can fix that. It's more for when you start to feel sleepy."

Blarik's thoughts wandered back to Swila. "Did she look happy?"

"Aye."

"So, what now?"

"Well, boy. We're taking on supplies. Seems Swila was the daughter of an influential man here in New Gradenbach. We have been given whatever we want for free. So, we're loading up on supplies and lumber. The only thing they won't let us do is hire crew."

"Where do we go from here?"

"Well, seems the city wants to hire us to go to an island that maps say isn't there. It supposedly is a floating island. They will allow us to fly under their flag and offered to pay us king's sum to find this island, search the ruins, and bring back some charm."

"What makes it so special?"

Tibbs shrugged and refilled their mugs. "Beats me, Blarik. But the task seems easy enough."

Blarik gulped down the rest of the coffee. "Pour me another, Mr. Tibbs. All this talk of adventure is really pepping me up."

They both had a hearty laugh.

GLOSSARY

Aboe (*uh-bow*): Tropical city state nation. Southern most kingdom on Terrigan.

Anxto (*Anks-toe*): Term used when describing something that is painful or tedious.

Blarik (*Blair-ick*): Minotaur born white on Kerisis. Captain Tarrar (*Tar-are*): Current Captain of the ship, Undaunted.

Elder Iska (*Iss-kuh*): A shaman elder skilled in the use of water based magic.

Erwo (*Air-woe*): Bag of grain, measured to be enough for one person for one day's rations. Glouwo (*Gl-ow-woe*): Blarik's father Jenison Gregor (*Jen-ih-son*): Priest of Surshy on the ship, Undaunted.

Kerisis (*Care-uh-siss*) The immense island were the minotaurs all live.

Kupona Grass (*Kue-poe-nuh*): Tall grass that covered much of the pains of Kerisis. Most commonly found near rivers and lake beds.

Kridja (*Krid-Juh*): Blarik's mother. Her nickname in the village is Jegina. (cold)

Lawo grass (*Lah-woe*): Type of grass found in flood plains. Much like wheat.

Mammo weed (*Ma'am-oh*): Milkweed that is native to Kerisis.

Morwen (*More-win*): A crab/spider like monster kept by Minotaur necromancers.

New Gradenbach (*Graud-in-bock*): Swila's home town.

Old Anku (*Onk-oo*): Necromancer from Blarik's tribe.

Oxtumeto (*Ox-too-met-oh*): Blarik's brother.

Rigjo (*Rig-joe*) The name taken by every tribe chief.

Skrull (*Skrull*): Large muskrat like creature on Kerisis. Extremely territorial.

Swila (Beatle): Blarik's human friend. Her real name is Kim. Tibbs

Variless: The- Tyrinian naval vessel that patrols southern waters from northern Aboe and Southern Tyrine.

Werito (earth): Blarik's grandfather

ABOUT THE AUTHOR

Shane Moore grew up on a farm in rural Illinois. An only child that was six miles from his nearest peer, Shane often created wild tales of heroes and villains during his many trips into the deep woods that surrounded his rural home.

Shane was accelerated in his class and started his senior year of high school at age sixteen. After graduating and getting a waiver for his age, Shane joined the United States Navy to pay for college. He participated in campaigns; "Provide Hope" and "Secure Democracy" during the Yugoslavian civil war. Shane received several naval awards and citations and was one of the highest trained members of his ship.

After getting out of the service, Shane began college. He was soon hired by the Carlinville Police Department, beginning his multiple venue police career. Shane retired as a detective for the Gillespie Police Department after serving twelve years. His police career was quite notable with awards for bravery and with one life saving medal. He was named Officer of the Year in 2005.

A lesser known truth about Shane is that he played eight years of semi pro football with the Central Illinois Cougars. Shane is the team's all-time tackle leader and holds the record for most special teams tackles in a season and the most tackles in a game. Shane received many awards including Defensive Player of the Year in 2005.

January 14th, 2008. Shane retires from his police career to be a professional novelist.

Mr. Moore resides in Central Illinois with his son, Dakota.

www.ingramcontent.com/pod-product-compliance
Lightning Source LLC
Chambersburg PA
CBHW060129260626
47160CB00005B/2052